T0145617

Hell

Hell
Henri Barbusse

MINT EDITIONS

Hell was first published in 1908.

This edition published by Mint Editions 2021.

ISBN 9781513283265 | E-ISBN 9781513288284

Published by Mint Editions®

MINT
EDITIONS

minteditionbooks.com

Publishing Director: Jennifer Newens
Design & Production: Rachel Lopez Metzger
Project Manager: Micaela Clark
Translated by: Edward J. O'Brien
Typesetting: Westchester Publishing Services

Contents

I

The landlady, Madame Lemercier, left me alone in my room, after a short speech impressing upon me all the material and moral advantages of the Lemercier boarding-house.

I stopped in front of the glass, in the middle of the room in which I was going to live for a while. I looked round the room and then at myself.

The room was grey and had a dusty smell. I saw two chairs, one of which held my valise, two narrow-backed armchairs with smeary upholstery, a table with a piece of green felt set into the top, and an oriental carpet with an arabesque pattern that fairly leaped to the eye.

This particular room I had never seen before, but, oh, how familiar it all was—that bed of imitation mahogany, that frigid toilet table, that inevitable arrangement of the furniture, that emptiness within those four walls.

The room was worn with use, as if an infinite number of people had occupied it. The carpet was frayed from the door to the window—a path trodden by a host of feet from day to day. The moulding, which I could reach with my hands, was out of line and cracked, and the marble mantelpiece had lost its sharp edges. Human contact wears things out with disheartening slowness.

Things tarnish, too. Little by little, the ceiling had darkened like a stormy sky. The places on the whitish woodwork and the pink wallpaper that had been touched oftenest had become smudgy—the edge of the door, the paint around the lock of the closet and the wall alongside the window where one pulls the curtain cords. A whole world of human beings had passed here like smoke, leaving nothing white but the window.

And I? I am a man like every other man, just as that evening was like every other evening.

I HAD BEEN TRAVELLING SINCE morning. Hurry, formalities, baggage, the train, the whiff of different towns.

I fell into one of the armchairs. Everything became quieter and more peaceful.

My coming from the country to stay in Paris for good marked an epoch in my life. I had found a situation here in a bank. My days were to change. It was because of this change that I got away from my usual thoughts and turned to thoughts of myself.

I was thirty years old. I had lost my father and mother eighteen or twenty years before, so long ago that the event was now insignificant. I was unmarried. I had no children and shall have none. There are moments when this troubles me, when I reflect that with me a line will end which has lasted since the beginning of humanity.

Was I happy? Yes, I had nothing to mourn or regret, I had no complicated desires. Therefore, I was happy. I remembered that since my childhood I had had spiritual illuminations, mystical emotions, a morbid fondness for shutting myself up face to face with my past. I had attributed exceptional importance to myself and had come to think that I was more than other people. But this had gradually become submerged in the positive nothingness of every day.

There I was now in that room.

I leaned forward in my armchair to be nearer the glass, and I examined myself carefully.

Rather short, with an air of reserve (although there are times when I let myself go); quite correctly dressed; nothing to criticise and nothing striking about my appearance.

I looked close at my eyes. They are green, though, oddly enough, people usually take them for black.

I believed in many things in a confused sort of way, above all, in the existence of God, if not in the dogmas of religion. However, I thought, these last had advantages for poor people and for women, who have less intellect than men.

As for philosophical discussions, I thought they are absolutely useless. You cannot demonstrate or verify anything. What was truth, anyway?

I had a sense of good and evil. I would not have committed an indelicacy, even if certain of impunity. I would not have permitted myself the slightest overstatement.

If everyone were like me, all would be well.

It was already late. I was not going to do anything. I remained seated there, at the end of the day, opposite the looking-glass. In the setting of the room that the twilight began to invade, I saw the outline of my forehead, the oval of my face, and, under my blinking eyelids, the gaze by which I enter into myself as into a tomb.

My tiredness, the gloominess (I heard rain outside), the darkness that intensified my solitude and made me look larger, and then something else, I knew not what, made me sad. It bored me to be sad. I shook myself. What was the matter? Nothing. Only myself.

I have not always been alone in life as I was that evening. Love for me had taken on the form and the being of my little Josette. We had met long before, in the rear of the millinery shop in which she worked at Tours. She had smiled at me with singular persistence, and I caught her head in my hands, kissed her on the lips—and found out suddenly that I loved her.

I no longer recall the strange bliss we felt when, we first embraced. It is true, there are moments when I still desire her as madly as the first time. This is so especially when she is away. When she is with me, there are moments when she repels me.

We discovered each other in the holidays. The days when we shall see each other again before we die—we could count them—if we dared.

To die! The idea of death is decidedly the most important of all ideas. I should die some day. Had I ever thought of it? I reflected. No, I had never thought of it. I could not. You can no more look destiny in the face than you can look at the sun, and yet destiny is grey.

And night came, as every night will come, until the last one, which will be too vast.

But all at once I jumped up and stood on my feet, reeling, my heart throbbing like the fluttering of wings.

What was it? In the street a horn resounded, playing a hunting song. Apparently some groom of a rich family, standing near the bar of a tavern, with cheeks puffed out, mouth squeezed tight, and an air of ferocity, astonishing and silencing his audience.

But the thing that so stirred me was not the mere blowing of a horn in the city streets. I had been brought up in the country, and as a child I used to hear that blast far in the distance, along the road to the woods and the castle. The same air, the same thing exactly. How could the two be so precisely alike?

And involuntarily my hand wavered to my heart.

Formerly—today—my life—my heart—myself! I thought of all this suddenly, for no reason, as if I had gone mad.

MY PAST—WHAT HAD I ever made of myself? Nothing, and I was already on the decline. Ah, because the refrain recalled the past, it seemed to me as if it were all over with me, and I had not lived. And I had a longing for a sort of lost paradise.

But of what avail to pray or rebel? I felt I had nothing more to expect from life. Thenceforth, I should be neither happy nor unhappy. I could not rise from the dead. I would grow old quietly, as quiet as I was that day in the room where so many people had left their traces, and yet no one had left his own traces.

This room—anywhere you turn, you find this room. It is the universal room. You think it is closed. No, it is open to the four winds of heaven. It is lost amid a host of similar rooms, like the light in the sky, like one day amid the host of all other days, like my "I" amid a host of other I's.

I, I! I saw nothing more now than the pallor of my face, with deep orbits, buried in the twilight, and my mouth filled with a silence which gently but surely stifles and destroys.

I raised myself on my elbow as on a clipped wing. I wished that something partaking of the infinite would happen to me.

I had no genius, no mission to fulfil, no great heart to bestow. I had nothing and I deserved nothing. But all the same I desired some sort of reward.

Love. I dreamed of a unique, an unheard-of idyll with a woman far from the one with whom I had hitherto lost all my time, a woman whose features I did not see, but whose shadow I imagined beside my own as we walked along the road together.

Something infinite, something new! A journey, an extraordinary journey into which to throw myself headlong and bring variety into my life. Luxurious, bustling departures surrounded by solicitous inferiors, a lazy leaning back in railway trains that thunder along through wild landscapes and past cities rising up and growing as if blown by the wind.

Steamers, masts, orders given in barbarous tongues, landings on golden quays, then strange, exotic faces in the sunlight, puzzlingly alike, and monuments, familiar from pictures, which, in my tourist's pride, seem to have come close to me.

My brain was empty, my heart arid. I had never found anything, not even a friend. I was a poor man stranded for a day in a boarding-house room where everybody comes and everybody goes. And yet I longed for glory! For glory bound to me like a miraculous wound that I should feel and everybody would talk about. I longed for a following of which I should be the leader, my name acclaimed under the heavens like a new clarion call.

But I felt my grandeur slip away. My childish imagination played in vain with those boundless fancies. There was nothing more for me to expect from life. There was only I, who, stripped by the night, rose upward like a cry.

I could hardly see any more in the dark. I guessed at, rather than saw, myself in the mirror. I had a realising sense of my weakness and captivity. I held my hands out toward the window, my outstretched fingers making them look like something torn. I lifted my face up to the sky. I sank back and leaned on the bed, a huge object with a vague human shape, like a corpse. God, I was lost! I prayed to Him to have pity on me. I thought that I was wise and content with my lot. I had said to myself that I was free from the instinct of theft. Alas, alas, it was not true, since I longed to take everything that was not mine.

II

The sound of the horn had ceased for some time. The street and the houses had quieted down. Silence. I passed my hand over my forehead. My fit of emotion was over. So much the better. I recovered my balance by an effort of will-power.

I sat down at the table and took some papers out of my bag that I had to look over and arrange.

Something spurred me on. I wanted to earn a little money. I could then send some to my old aunt who had brought me up. She always waited for me in the low-ceilinged room, where her sewing-machine, afternoons, whirred, monotonous and tiresome as a clock, and where, evenings, there was a lamp beside her which somehow seemed to look like herself.

Notes—the notes from which I was to draw up the report that would show my ability and definitely decide whether I would get a position in Monsieur Berton's bank—Monsieur Berton, who could do everything for me, who had but to say a word, the god of my material life.

I started to light the lamp. I scratched a match. It did not catch fire, the phosphorous end breaking off. I threw it away and waited a moment, feeling a little tired.

Then I heard a song hummed quite close to my ear.

SOME ONE SEEMED TO BE leaning on my shoulder, singing for me, only for me, in confidence.

Ah, an hallucination! Surely my brain was sick—my punishment for having thought too hard.

I stood up, and my hand clutched the edge of the table. I was oppressed by a feeling of the supernatural. I sniffed the air, my eyelids blinking, alert and suspicious.

The singing kept on. I could not get rid of it. My head was beginning to go round. The singing came from the room next to mine. Why was it so pure, so strangely near? Why did it touch me so? I looked at the wall between the two rooms, and stifled a cry of surprise.

High up, near the ceiling, above the door, always kept locked, there was a light. The song fell from that star.

There was a crack in the partition at that spot, through which the light of the next room entered the night of mine.

I climbed up on the bed, and my face was on a level with the crack. Rotten woodwork, two loose bricks. The plaster gave way and an opening appeared as large as my hand, but invisible from below, because of the moulding.

I looked. I beheld. The next room presented itself to my sight freely.

It spread out before me, this room which was not mine. The voice that had been singing had gone, and in going had left the door open, and it almost seemed as though the door were still swinging on its hinges. There was nothing in the room but a lighted candle, which trembled on the mantelpiece.

At that distance the table looked like an island, the bluish and reddish pieces of furniture, in their vague outline, like the organs of a body almost alive.

I looked at the wardrobe. Bright, confused lines going straight up, its feet in darkness. The ceiling, the reflection of the ceiling in the glass, and the pale window like a human face against the sky.

I returned to my room—as if I had really left it—stunned at first, my thoughts in a whirl, almost forgetting who I was.

I sat down on my bed, thinking things over quickly and trembling a little, oppressed by what was to come.

I dominated, I possessed that room. My eyes entered it. I was in it. All who would be there would be there with me without knowing it. I should see them, I should hear them, I should be as much in their company as though the door were open.

A MOMENT LATER I RAISED my face to the hole and looked again.

The candle was out, but some one was there. It was the maid. No doubt she had come in to put the room in order. Then she paused.

She was alone. She was quite near me. But I did not very well see the living being who was moving about, perhaps because I was dazzled by seeing it so truly—a dark blue apron, falling down from her waist like rays of evening, white wrists, hands darker than her wrists from toil, a face undecided yet striking, eyes hidden yet shining, cheeks prominent and clear, a knot on top of her head gleaming like a crown.

A short time before I had seen the girl on the staircase bending over cleaning the banisters, her reddened face close to her large hands. I had found her repulsive because of those blackened hands of hers and the dusty chores that she stooped over. I had also seen her in a hallway walking ahead of me heavily, her hair hanging loose and her body giving out an unpleasant odour, so that you felt it was obnoxious and wrapped in dirty underwear.

A<small>ND NOW</small> I <small>LOOKED AT</small> her again. The evening gently dispelled the ugliness, wiped out the misery and the horror, changed the dust into shadow, like a curse turned into a blessing. All that remained of her was colour, a mist, an outline; not even that; a thrill and the beating of her heart. Every trace of her had disappeared save her true self.

That was because she was alone. An extraordinary thing, a dash of the divine in it, to be actually alone. She was in that perfect innocence, that purity which is solitude.

I desecrated her solitude with my eyes, but she did not know it, and so *she* was not desecrated.

She went over to the window with brightening eyes and swinging hands in her apron of the colour of the nocturnal sky. Her face and the upper part of her body were illuminated. She seemed to be in heaven.

She sat down on the sofa, a great low red shadow in the depths of the room near the window. She leaned her broom beside her. Her dust cloth fell to the floor and was lost from sight.

She took a letter from her pocket and read it. In the twilight the letter was the whitest thing in the world. The double sheet trembled between her fingers, which held it carefully, like a dove in the air. She put the trembling letter to her lips, and kissed it. From whom was the letter? Not from her family. A servant girl is not likely to have so much filial devotion as to kiss a letter from her parents. A lover, her betrothed, yes. Many, perhaps, knew her lover's name. I did not, but I witnessed her love as no other person had. And that simple gesture of kissing the paper, that gesture buried in a room, stripped bare by the dark, had something sublime and awesome in it.

She rose and went closer to the window, the white letter folded in her grey hand.

The night thickened—and it seemed to me as if I no longer knew her age, nor her name, nor the work she happened to be doing down here, nor anything about her—nothing at all. She gazed at the pale immensity, which touched her. Her eyes gleamed. You would say she was crying, but no, her eyes only shed light. She would be an angel if reality flourished upon the earth.

She sighed and walked to the door slowly. The door closed behind her like something falling.

She had gone without doing anything but reading her letter and kissing it.

I RETURNED TO MY CORNER lonely, more terribly alone than before. The simplicity of this meeting stirred me profoundly. Yet there had been no one there but a human being, a human being like myself. Then there is nothing sweeter and stronger than to approach a human being, whoever that human being may be.

This woman entered into my intimate life and took a place in my heart. How? Why? I did not know. But what importance she assumed! Not of herself. I did not know her, and I did not care to know her. She assumed importance by the sole value of the momentary revelation of her existence, by the example she gave, by the wake of her actual presence, by the true sound of her steps.

It seemed to me as if the supernatural dream I had had a short while before had been granted, and that what I called the infinite had come. What that woman, without knowing it, had given me by showing me her naked kiss—was it not the crowning beauty the reflection of which covers you with glory?

THE DINNER BELL RANG.

This summons to everyday reality and one's usual occupations changed the course of my thoughts for the moment. I got ready to go down to dinner. I put on a gay waistcoat and a dark coat, and I stuck a pearl in my cravat. Then I stood still and listened, hoping to hear a footstep or a voice.

While doing these conventional things, I continued to be obsessed by the great event that had happened—this apparition.

I went downstairs and joined the rest of my fellow-boarders in the brown and gold dining-room. There was a general stir and bustle and the usual empty interest before a meal. A number of people seated themselves with the good manners of polite society. Smiles, the sound of chairs being drawn up to the table, words thrown out, conversations started. Then the concert of plates and dishes began and grew steadily louder.

My neighbours talked to those beside them. I heard their murmur, which accentuated my aloneness. I lifted my eyes. In front of me a shining row of foreheads, eyes, collars, shirtfronts, waists, and busy hands above a table of glistening whiteness. All these things attracted my attention and distracted it at the same time.

I did not know what these people were thinking about. I did not know who they were. They hid themselves from one another. Their shining fronts made a wall against which I dashed in vain.

Bracelets, necklaces, rings. The sparkling of the jewels made me feel far away from them as do the stars. A young girl looked at me with vague blue eyes. What could I do against that kind of sapphire?

They talked, but the noise left each one to himself, and deafened me, as the light blinded me.

Nevertheless, at certain moments these people, because in the course of conversation they thought of things they had at heart, revealed themselves as if they were alone. I recognized the revelation of this truth, and felt myself turning pale on remembering that other revelation.

Some one spoke of money, and the subject became general. The assembly was stirred by an ideal. A dream of grasping and touching shone through their eyes, just as a little adoration had come into the eyes of the servant when she found herself alone.

They recalled military heroes triumphantly, and some men thought, "Me, too!" and worked themselves up into a fever, showing what they were thinking of, in spite of their ridiculously low station and the slavery of their social position. One young girl seemed dazzled, looked overwhelmed. She could not restrain a sigh of ecstasy. She blushed under the effect of an inscrutable thought. I saw the surge of blood mount to her face. I saw her heart beaming.

They discussed the phenomena of occultism and the Beyond. "Who knows?" some one said. Then they discussed death. Two diners, at opposite ends of the table, a man and a woman who had not spoken to each other and seemed not to be acquainted, exchanged a glance that I caught. And seeing that glance leap from their eyes at the same time, under the shock of the idea of death, I understood that these two loved each other.

THE MEAL WAS OVER. THE young people went into the parlour. A lawyer was telling some people around him about a murder case that had been decided that day. The nature of the subject was such that he expressed himself very cautiously, as though confiding a secret. A man had injured and then murdered a little girl and had kept singing at the top of his voice to prevent the cries of his little victim from being heard. One by one the people stopped talking and listened with the air of really not listening, while those not so close to the speaker felt like drawing up right next to him. About this image risen in their midst, this paroxysm so frightful to our timid instincts, the silence spread in a circle in their souls like a terrific noise.

Then I heard the laugh of a woman, of an honest woman, a dry crackling laugh, which she thought innocent perhaps, but which caressed her whole being, a burst of laughter, which, made up of formless instinctive cries, was almost fleshy. She stopped and turned, silent again. And the speaker, sure of his effect, continued in a calm voice to hurl upon these people the story of the monster's confession.

A young mother, whose daughter was sitting beside her, half got up, but could not leave. She sat down again and bent forward to conceal her daughter. She was eager and yet ashamed to listen.

Another woman was sitting motionless, with her head leaning forward, but her mouth compressed as if she were defending herself tragically. And beneath the worldly mask of her face, I saw a fanatical martyr's smile impress itself like handwriting.

And the men! I distinctly heard one man, the man who was so calm and simple, catch his breath. Another man, with a characterless business man's face, was making a great effort to talk of this and that to a young girl sitting next to him, while he watched her with a look of which he was ashamed and which made him blink. And everybody condemned the satyr in terms of the greatest abuse.

And so, for a moment, they had not lied. They had almost confessed, perhaps unconsciously, and even without knowing what they had confessed. They had almost been their real selves. Desire had leaped into their eyes, and the reflection passed—and I had seen what happened in the silence, sealed by their lips.

It is this, it is this thought, this kind of living spectre, that I wished to study. I rose, shrugging my shoulders, and hurried out, impelled by eagerness to see the sincerity of men and women unveiled before my eyes, beautiful as a masterpiece in spite of its ugliness. So, back in my room again, I placed myself against the wall as if to embrace it and look down into the Room.

There it was at my feet. Even when empty, it was more alive than the people one meets and associates with, the people who have the vastness of numbers to lose themselves in and be forgotten in, who have voices for lying and faces to hide themselves behind.

III

Night, absolute night. Shadows thick as velvet hung all around. Everything sank into darkness. I sat down and leaned my elbow on the round table, lighted by the lamp. I meant to work, but as a matter of fact I only listened.

I had looked into the Room a short time before. No one had been there, but no doubt some one was going to come.

Some one was going to come, that evening perhaps, or the next day, or the day after. Some one was bound to come. Then other human beings would follow in succession. I waited, and it seemed to me as if that was all I was made for.

I waited a long time, not daring to go to sleep. Then, very late, when silence had been reigning so long that it paralysed me, I made an effort. I leaned up against the wall once more and looked prayerfully. The Room was black, all things blending into one, full of the night, full of the unknown, of every possible thing. I dropped back into my own room.

The next day I saw the Room in the simplicity of daylight. I saw the dawn spread over it. Little by little, it began to come out of its ruins and to rise.

It was arranged and furnished on the same plan as my own room. Opposite me was the mantelpiece with the looking-glass above. On the right was the bed, and on the left, on the same side as the window, a sofa, chairs, armchairs, table, wardrobe. The rooms were identical, but the history of mine was finished while the history of the other one had not yet begun.

After an insipid breakfast, I returned to the spot that attracted me, the hole in the partition. Nothing. I climbed down again.

It was close. A faint smell from the kitchen lingered even here. I paused in the infinite vastness of my empty room.

I opened my door a little bit, then all the way. In the hall the door of each room was painted brown, with numbers carved on brass plates. All were closed. I took a few steps, which I alone heard—heard echoing too loudly in that house, huge and immobile.

The passage was very long and narrow. The wall was hung with imitation tapestry of dark green foliage, against which shone the copper of a gas fixture. I leaned over the banister. A servant (the one who waited at the table and was wearing a blue apron now, hardly recognisable with her hair in disorder) came skipping down from the floor above with newspapers under her arm. Madame Lemercier's little girl, with a careful hand on the banister, was coming upstairs, her neck thrust forward like a bird, and I compared her little footsteps to fragments of passing seconds. A lady and a gentleman passed in front of me, breaking off their conversation to keep me from catching what they were saying, as if they refused me the alms of their thoughts.

These trifling events disappeared like scenes of a comedy on which the curtain falls.

I passed the whole afternoon disheartened. I felt as if I were alone against them all, while roaming about inside this house and yet outside of it.

As I passed through the hallway, a door went shut hastily, cutting off the laugh of a woman taken by surprise. A senseless noise oozed from the walls, worse than silence. From under each door a broken ray of light crept out, worse than darkness.

I went downstairs to the parlour, attracted by the sound of conversation.

A group of men were talking, I no longer remember about what. They went out, and I was alone. I heard them talking in the hall. Then their voices died away.

A fashionable lady came in, with a rustle of silk and the smell of flowers and perfume. She took up a lot of room because of her fragrance and elegance. She carried her head held slightly forward and had a beautiful long face set off by an expression of great sweetness. But I could not see her well, because she did not look at me. She seated herself, picked up a book, and turned the pages, and the leaves cast upon her face a reflection of whiteness and thoughtfulness.

I watched her bosom rising and falling, and her motionless face, and the living book that was merged with her. Her complexion was so brilliant that her mouth seemed almost dark. Her beauty saddened me. I looked at this unknown woman with sublime regret. She caressed me by her presence. A woman always caresses a man when she comes near him and they are alone. In spite of all sorts of separation, there is always an awful beginning of happiness between them.

But she went out. That was the end of her. Nothing had happened, and now it was over. All this was too simple, too hard, too true.

A gentle despair that I had never experienced before troubled me. Since the previous day I had changed. Human life, its living truth, I knew it as we all know it. I had been familiar with it all my life. I believed in it with a kind of fear now that it had appeared to me in a divine form.

IV

I went for several days without seeing anything. Those days were frightfully warm. At first the sky was grey and rainy. Now September was flaming to a close. Friday! Why, I had been in that house a week already.

One sultry morning I sat in my room and sank into dreamy musings and thought of a fairy tale.

The edge of a forest. In the undergrowth on the dark emerald carpet, circles of sunlight. Below, a hill rising from the plain, and above the thick yellow and dark-green foliage, a bit of wall and a turret as in a tapestry. A page advanced dressed like a bird. A buzzing. It was the sound of the royal chase in the distance. Unusually pleasant things were going to happen.

THE NEXT AFTERNOON WAS ALSO hot and sunny. I remembered similar afternoons, years before and the present seemed to be that past, as if the glowing heat had effaced time and had stifled all other days beneath its brooding wings.

The room next to mine was almost dark. They had closed the shutters. Through the double curtains made out of some thin material I saw the window streaked with shining bars, like the grating in front of a fire.

In the torrid silence of the house, in the large slumber it enclosed, bursts of laughter mounted and broke, voices died away, as they had the day before and as they always would.

From out of these remoter sounds emerged the distinct sound of footsteps, coming nearer and nearer. I propped myself up against the wall and looked. The door of the Room opened, as if pushed in by the flood of light that streamed through it, and two tiny shadows appeared, engulfed in the brightness.

They acted as though they were being pursued. They hesitated on the threshold, the doorway making a frame around those little creatures. And then they entered.

The door closed. The Room was now alive. I scrutinised the newcomers. I saw them indistinctly through the dark red and green spots dancing in front of my eyes, which had been dazzled by the flood of light. A little boy and a little girl, twelve or thirteen years old.

They sat down on the sofa, and looked at each other in silence. Their faces were almost alike.

THE BOY MURMURED:

"You see, Hélène, there is no one here."

And a hand pointed to the uncovered bed, and to the empty table and empty clothes-racks—the careful denudation of unoccupied rooms.

Then the same hand began to tremble like a leaf. I heard the beating of my heart. The voices whispered:

"We are alone. They did not see us."

"This is about the first time we've ever been alone together."

"Yet we have always known each other."

A little laugh.

They seemed to need solitude, the first step to a mystery toward which they were travelling together. They had fled from the others. They had created for themselves the forbidden solitude. But you could clearly tell that now that they had found solitude, they did not know what else to look for.

THEN I HEARD ONE OF them stammer and say sadly, with almost a sob:

"We love each other dearly."

Then a tender phrase rose breathlessly, groping for words, timidly, like a bird just learning to fly:

"I'd like to love you more."

To see them thus bent toward each other, in the warm shadow, which bathed them and veiled the childishness of their features, you would have thought them two lovers meeting.

Two lovers! That was their dream, though they did not yet know what love meant.

One of them had said "the first time." It was the time that they felt they were alone, although these two cousins had been living close together.

No doubt it was the first time that the two had sought to leave friendship and childhood behind them. It was the first time that desire had come to surprise and trouble two hearts, which until now had slept.

SUDDENLY THEY STOOD UP, AND the slender ray of sunlight, which passed over them and fell at their feet, revealed their figures, lighted up their faces and hair, so that their presence brightened the room.

Were they going away? No, they sat down again. Everything fell back into shadow, into mystery, into truth.

HENRI BARBUSSE

In beholding them, I felt a confused mingling of my past and the past of the world. Where were they? Everywhere, since they existed. They were on the banks of the Nile, the Ganges, or the Cydnus, on the banks of the eternal river of the ages. They were Daphnis and Chloë, under a myrtle bush, in the Greek sunshine, the shimmer of leaves on their faces, and their faces mirroring each other. Their vague little conversation hummed like the wings of a bee, near the freshness of fountains and the heat that consumed the meadows, while in the distance a chariot went by, laden with sheaves.

The new world opened. The panting truth was there. It confused them. They feared the brusque intrusion of some divinity. They were happy and unhappy. They nestled as close together as they could. They brought to each other as much as they could. But they did not suspect what it was that they were bringing. They were too small, too young. They had not lived long enough. Each was to self a stifling secret.

Like all human beings, like me, like us, they wished for what they did not have. They were beggars. But they asked *themselves* for charity. They asked for help from their *own* persons.

The boy, a man already, impoverished already by his feminine companion, turned, drawn towards her, and held out his awkward arms, without daring to look at her.

The girl, a woman already, leaned her face on the back of the sofa, her eyes shining. Her cheeks were plump and rosy, tinted and warmed by her heart. The skin of her neck, taut and satiny, quivered. Half-blown and waiting, a little voluptuous because voluptuousness already emanated from her, she was like a rose inhaling sunlight.

And I—I could not tear my eyes from them.

AFTER A LONG SILENCE, HE murmured:

"Shall we stop calling each other by our first names?"

"Why?"

He seemed absorbed in thought.

"So as to begin over again," he said at last.

"Shall we, Miss Janvier?" he asked again.

She gave a visible start at the touch of this new manner of address, at the word "Miss," as if it were a kind of embrace.

"Why, Mr. Lecoq," she ventured hesitatingly, "it is as though something had covered us, and we were removing—"

Now, he became bolder.

"Shall we kiss each other on our mouths?"

She was oppressed, and could not quite smile.

"Yes," she said.

They caught hold of each other's arms and shoulders and held out their lips, as if their mouths were birds.

"Jean!" "Hélène!" came softly.

It was the first thing they had found out. To embrace the embracer, is it not the tiniest caress and the least sort of a bond? And yet it is so sternly prohibited.

Again they seemed to me to be without age.

They were like all lovers, while they held hands, their faces joined, trembling and blind, in the shadow of a kiss.

THEY BROKE OFF, AND DISENGAGED themselves from their embrace, whose meaning they had not yet learned.

They talked with their innocent lips. About what? About the past, which was so near and so short.

They were leaving their paradise of childhood and ignorance. They spoke of a house and a garden where they had both lived.

The house absorbed them. It was surrounded by a garden wall, so that from the road all you could see was the tip of the eaves, and you couldn't tell what was going on inside of it.

They prattled:

"The rooms, when we were little and they were so big—"

"It was easier to walk there than anywhere else."

To hear the children talk, you would have thought there was something benevolent and invisible, something like the good God of the past, behind those walls. She hummed an air she had heard there, and said that music was easier to remember than people. They dropped back into the past easily and naturally. They wrapped themselves up in their memories as though they were cold.

"The other day, just before we left, I took a candle and walked alone through the rooms, which scarcely woke up to watch me pass."

In the garden, so prim and well kept, they thought only of the flowers, and little else. They saw the pool, the shady walk, and the cherry tree, which, in winter when the lawn was white, they made believe had too many blossoms—snow blossoms.

The day before they had still been in the garden, like brother and sister. Now life seemed to have grown serious all at once, and they no

HENRI BARBUSSE

longer knew how to play. I saw that they wanted to kill the past. When we are old, we let it die; when we are young and strong, we kill it.

She sat up straight.

"I don't want to remember any more," she said.

And he:

"I don't want us to be like each other any more. I don't want us to be brother and sister any more."

Gradually their eyes opened.

"To touch nothing but each other's hands," he muttered, trembling.

"Brother—sister—that's nothing."

It had come—the hour of beautiful, troubled decisions, of forbidden fruits. They had not belonged to each other before. The hour had come when they sought to be all in all to each other.

They were a little self-conscious, a little ashamed of themselves already. A few days before, in the evening, it had given them profound pleasure to disobey their parents and go out of the garden although they had been forbidden to leave it.

"Grandmother came to the top of the steps and called to us to come in."

"But we were gone. We had slipped through the hole in the hedge where a bird always sang. There was no wind, and scarcely any light. Even the trees didn't stir. The dust on the ground was dead. The shadows stole round us so softly that we almost spoke to them. We were frightened to see night coming on. Everything had lost its colour. But the night was clear, and the flowers, the road, even the wheat were silver. And it was then that my mouth came closest to your mouth."

"The night," she said, her soul carried aloft on a wave of beauty, "the night caresses the caresses."

"I took your hand, and I knew that you would live life whole. When I used to say 'Hélène,' I did not know what I was saying. Now, when I shall say 'she,' it will be everything."

Once more their lips joined. Their mouths and their eyes were those of Adam and Eve. I recalled the ancestral lesson from which sacred history and human history flow as from a fountain. They wandered in the penetrating light of paradise without knowledge. They were as if they did not exist. When—through triumphant curiosity, though forbidden by God himself—they learned the secret, the sky was darkened. The certainty of a future of sorrow had fallen upon them. Angels pursued them like vultures. They grovelled on the ground from day to day, but they had created love, they had replaced divine riches by the poverty of belonging to each other.

The two little children had taken their parts in the eternal drama. By talking to each other as they did they had restored to their first names their full significance.

"I should like to love you more. I should like to love you harder. How could I?"

THEY SAID NO MORE, AS though there were no more words for them. They were completely absorbed in themselves, and their hands trembled.

Then they rose, and as they did so, the door opened. There stood the old stooping grandmother. She came out of the grey, out of the realm of phantoms, out of the past. She was looking for them as if they had gone astray. She called them in a low voice. She put into her tone a great gentleness, almost sadness, strangely harmonising with the children's presence.

"You are here, children?" she said, with a kind little laugh. "What are you doing here? Come, they are looking for you."

She was old and faded, but she was angelic, with her gown fastened up to her neck. Beside these two, who were preparing for the large life, she was, thenceforth, like a child, inactive, useless.

They rushed into her arms, and pressed their foreheads against her saintly mouth. They seemed to be saying good-by to her forever.

SHE WENT OUT. AND A moment afterwards they followed her, hastily, as they had come, united now by an invisible and sublime bond. On the threshold, they looked at each other once more.

And now that the room was empty like a deserted sanctuary, I thought of their glance, their first glance of love, which I had seen.

No one before me had ever seen a first glance of love. I was beside them, but, far away. I understood and read it without being part of the infatuation myself, without being lost in the sensation. That is why I saw that glance. They did not know when it began, they did not know that it was the first. Afterwards they would forget. The urgent flowering of their hearts would destroy those preludes. We can no more know our first glance of love than our last. I shall remember it when they will have forgotten it.

I do not recall my own first glance of love, my own first gift of love. Yet it happened. Those divine simplicities are erased from my heart.

Good God, then what do I retain that is of value? The little boy that I was is dead forever, before my eyes. I survived him, but forgetfulness tormented me, then overcame me, the sad process of living ruined me, and I scarcely know what he knew. I remember things at random only, but the most beautiful, the sweetest memories are gone.

Well, this tender canticle that I overheard, full of infinity and overflowing with fresh laughter, this precious song, I take and hold and cherish. It pulses in my heart. I have stolen, but I have preserved truth.

V

For a day, the Room remained vacant. Twice I had high hopes, then disillusionment.

Waiting had become a habit, an occupation. I put off appointments, delayed my walks, gained time at the risk of losing my position. I arranged my life as for a new love. I left my room only to go down to dinner, where nothing interested me any more.

The second day, I noticed that the Room was ready to receive a new occupant. It was waiting. I had a thousand dreams of who the guest would be, while the Room kept its secret, like some one thinking.

Twilight came, then evening, which magnified the room but did not change it. I was already in despair, when the door opened in the darkness, and I saw on the threshold the shadow of a man.

He was scarcely to be distinguished in the evening light.

Dark clothing, milky white cuffs from which his grey tapering hands hung down; a collar a little whiter than the rest. In his round greyish face I could see the dusky hollows of his eyes and mouth, under the chin a cavity of shadow. The yellow of his forehead shone unclearly. His cheekbone made an obscure bar in the dusk. You would have called him a skeleton. What was this being whose physiognomy was so monstrously simple?

He came nearer, and his face kindled, assumed life. I saw that he was handsome.

He had a charming serious face, fringed with a fine black beard, a high forehead and sparkling eyes. A haughty grace guided and refined his movements.

He came forward a step or two, then returned to the door, which was still open. The shadow of the door trembled, a silhouette appeared and took shape. A little black-gloved hand grasped the knob, and a woman stole into the room, with a questioning face.

She must have been a few steps behind him in the street. They had not wished to enter the room together, in which they both sought refuge to escape pursuit.

She closed the door, and leaned her whole weight against it, to close it still tighter. Slowly she turned her head to him, paralysed for a moment, it seemed to me, with fear that it was not he. They stared into each other's faces. A cry burst from them, passionate, restrained, almost mute, echoing from one to the other. It seemed to open up their wound.

"You!"

"You!"

She almost fainted. She dropped on his breast as though swept by a storm. She had just strength enough to fall into his arms. I saw the man's two large pale hands, opened but slightly crooked, resting on the woman's back. A sort of desperate palpitation seized them, as if an immense angel were in the Room, struggling and making vain efforts to escape. And it seemed to me that the Room was too small for this couple, although it was full of the evening.

"They didn't see us!"

It was the same phrase which had come the other day from the two children.

He said, "Come!" leading her over to the sofa, near the window, and they seated themselves on the red velvet. I saw their arms joined together as though by a cord. They remained there, engrossed, gathering about them all the shadow of the world, reviving, beginning to live again in their element of night and solitude.

What an entry, what an entry! What an irruption of anathema!

I had thought, when this form of sin presented itself before me, when the woman appeared at the door, plainly driven toward him, that I should witness bliss in its plenitude, a savage and animal joy, as momentous as nature. On the contrary, I found that this meeting was like a heart-rending farewell.

"Then we shall always be afraid?"

She seemed just a little more tranquil, and said this with an anxious glance at him, as if really expecting a reply.

She shuddered, huddled in the shadows, feverishly stroking and pressing the man's hand, sitting upright, stiffly. I saw her throat rising and falling like the sea. They stayed there, touching one another; but a lingering terror mingled with their caresses.

"Always afraid—always afraid, always. Far from the street, far from the sun, far from everything. I who had so much wanted full daylight and sunlight!" she said, looking at the sky.

They were afraid. Fear moulded them, burrowed into their hearts. Their eyes, their hearts were afraid. Above all, their love was afraid.

A mournful smile glided across the man's face. He looked at his friend and murmured:

"You are thinking of *him*."

She was sitting with her cheeks in her hands and her elbows on her knees and her face thrust forward. She did not reply.

She *was* thinking of him. Doubled up, small as a child, she gazed intently into the distance, at the man who was not there. She bowed to this image like a suppliant, and felt a divine reflection from it falling upon her—from the man who was not there, who was being deceived, from the offended man, the wounded man, from the master, from him who was everywhere except where they were, who occupied the immense outside, and whose name made them bow their heads, the man to whom they were a prey.

Night fell, as if shame and terror were in its shadows, over this man and woman, who had come to hide their embraces in this room, as in a tomb where dwells the Beyond.

He said to her:

"I love you!"

I distinctly heard those grand words.

I love you! I shuddered to the depths of my being on hearing the profound words which came from those two human beings. I love you! The words which offer body and soul, the great open cry of the creature and the creation. I love you! I beheld love face to face.

Then it seemed to me that sincerity vanished in the hasty incoherent things he next said while clasping her to him. It was as though he had a set speech to make and was in a hurry to get through with it.

"You and I were born for each other. There is a kinship in our souls which must triumph. It was no more possible to prevent us from meeting and belonging to each other than to prevent our lips from uniting when they came together. What do moral conventions or social barriers matter to us? Our love is made of infinity and eternity."

"Yes," she said, lulled by his voice.

But I knew he was lying or was letting his words run away with him. Love had become an idol, a thing. He was blaspheming, he was invoking infinity and eternity in vain, paying lip service to it by daily prayer that had become perfunctory.

They let the banality drop. The woman remained pensive for a while, then she shook her head and she—*she* pronounced the word of excuse, of glorification; more than that, the word of truth:

"I was so unhappy!"

"How long ago it was!" she began.

It was her work of art, her poem and her prayer, to repeat this story, low and precipitately, as if she were in the confessional. You felt that she came to it quite naturally, without transition, so completely did it possess her whenever they were alone.

She was simply dressed. She had removed her black gloves and her coat and hat. She wore a dark skirt and a red waist upon which a thin gold chain was hanging.

She was a woman of thirty, perhaps, with regular features and smooth silken hair. It seemed to me that I knew her, but could not place her.

She began to speak of herself quite loudly, and tell of her past which had been so hard.

"What a life I led! What monotony, what emptiness! The little town, our house, the drawing-room with the furniture always arranged just so, their places never changed, like tombstones. One day I tried to put the table that stood in the centre in another place. I could not do it."

Her face paled, grew more luminous.

He listened to her. A smile of patience and resignation, which soon was like a pained expression of weariness, crept across his handsome face. Yes, he was really handsome, though a little disconcerting, with his large eyes, which women must have adored, his drooping moustache, his tender, distant air. He seemed to be one of those gentle people who think too much and do evil. You would have said that he was above everything and capable of everything. Listening to her with a certain remoteness, but stirred by desire for her, he had the air of waiting.

And suddenly the veil fell from my eyes, and reality lay stripped before me. I saw that between these two people there was an immense difference, like an infinite discord, sublime to behold because of its depths, but so painful that it bruised my heart.

He was moved only by his longing for her; *she*, by her need of escaping from her ordinary life. Their desires were not the same. They seemed united, but they dwelt far apart.

They did not talk the same language. When they spoke of the same things, they scarcely understood each other, and to my eyes, from the very first, their union appeared to be broken more than if they had never known each other.

But he did not say what was really in his mind. You felt it in the sound of his voice, the very charm of his intonation, his lyrical choice of words. He thought to please her, and he lied. He was evidently her superior, but she dominated him by a kind of inspired sincerity. While he was master of his words, she offered her whole self in her words.

She described her former life.

"From the windows in my room and the dining-room, I could look out on the square. The fountain in the centre, with its shadow at its base. I watched the day go round there, on that little, white, round place, like a sundial.

"The postman crossed it regularly, without thinking. At the arsenal gate stood a soldier doing nothing. Nobody else ever came there. When noon rang like a knell, still no one. What I remember best of all was the way noon rang like a knell—the middle of the day, absolute ennui.

"Nothing ever happened to me, nothing ever would happen to me. There was nothing for me. The future no longer existed for me. If my days were to go on like that, nothing would separate me from my death—nothing! Not a thing! To be bored is to die! My life was dead, and yet I had to live. It was suicide. Others killed themselves with poison or with a revolver. I killed myself with minutes and hours."

"Amy!" said the man.

"Then, by dint of seeing the days born in the morning and miscarrying in the evening, I became afraid to die, and this fear was my first passion.

"Often, in the middle of a visit I was paying, or in the night, or when I came home after a walk, the length of the convent wall, I shuddered with hope because of this passion.

"But who would free me from it? Who would save me from this invisible shipwreck, which I perceived only from time to time? Around me was a sort of conspiracy, composed of envy, meanness and indifference. Whatever I saw, whatever I heard, tended to throw me back into the narrow road, that stupid narrow road along which I was going.

"Madame Martet, the one friend with whom I was a little bit intimate, you know, only two years older than I am, told me that I must be content with what I had. I replied, 'Then, that is the end of everything, if I must be content with what I have. Do you really believe what you say?' She said she did. Oh, the horrid woman!

"But it was not enough to be afraid. I had to hate my ennui. How did I come to hate it? I do not know.

"I no longer knew myself. I no longer was myself. I had such need of something else. In fact, I did not know my own name any more.

"One day, I remember (although I am not wicked) I had a happy dream that my husband was dead, my poor husband who had done nothing to me, and that I was free, free, as large as the world!

"It could not last. I couldn't go on forever hating monotony so much. Oh, that emptiness, that monotony! Of all the gloomy things in the world monotony is the darkest, the gloomiest. In comparison night is day.

"Religion? It is not with religion that we fill the emptiness of our days, it is with our own life. It was not with beliefs, with ideas that I had to struggle, it was with myself.

"Then I found the remedy!"

She almost cried, hoarsely, ecstatically:

"Sin, sin! To rid myself of boredom by committing a crime, to break up monotony by deceiving. To sin in order to be a new person, another person. To hate life worse than it hated me. To sin so as not to die.

"I met you. You wrote verses and books. You were different from the rest. Your voice vibrated and gave the impression of beauty, and above all, you were there, in my existence, in front of me! I had only to hold out my arms. Then I loved you with all my heart, if you can call it love, my poor little friend!"

She spoke now in a low quick voice, both oppressed and enthusiastic, and she played with her companion's hand as if it were a child's toy.

"And you, too, you loved me, naturally. And when we slipped into a hotel one evening, the first time, it seemed to me as if the door opened of itself, and I was grateful for having rebelled and having broken my destiny. And then the deceit—from which we suffer sometimes, but which, after reflection, we no longer detest—the risks, the dangers that give pleasure to each minute, the complications that add variety to life, these rooms, these hiding-places, these black prisons, which have fled from the sunlight I once knew!

"Ah!" she said.

It seemed to me that she sighed as if, now that her aspiration was realized, she had nothing so beautiful to hope for any more.

SHE THOUGHT A MOMENT, AND then said:

"See what we are. I too may have believed at first in a sort of thunderbolt, a supernatural and fatal attraction, because of your poetry. But in reality I came to you—I see myself now—with clenched fists and closed eyes."

She added:

"We deceive ourselves a good deal about love. It is almost never what they say it is.

"There may be sublime affinities, magnificent attractions. I do not say such a love may not exist between two human beings. But we are not these two. We have never thought of anything but ourselves. I know, of course, that I am in love with you. So are you with me. There is an attraction for you which does not exist for me, since I do not feel any pleasure. You see, we are making a bargain. You give me a dream, I give you joy. But all this is not love."

He shrugged his shoulders, half in doubt, half in protest. He did not want to say anything. All the same, he murmured feebly:

"Even in the purest of loves we cannot escape from ourselves."

"Oh," she said with a gesture of pious protest, the vehemence of which surprised me, "that is not the same thing. Don't say that, don't say that!"

It seemed to me there was a vague regret in her voice and the dream of a new dream in her eyes.

She dispelled it with a shake of her head.

"How happy I was! I felt rejuvenated, like a new being. I had a sense of modesty again. I remember that I did not dare to show the tip of my foot from under my dress. I even had a feeling about my face, my hands, my very name."

Then the man continued the confession from the point where she had left off, and spoke of their first meetings. He wished to caress her with words, to win her over gradually with phrases and with the charm of memories.

"The first time we were alone—"

She looked at him.

"It was in the street, one evening," he said. "I took your arm. You leaned more and more upon my shoulder. People swarmed around us, but we seemed to be quite alone. Everything around us changed into absolute solitude. It seemed to me that we were both walking on the waves of the sea."

"Ah!" she said. "How good you were! That first evening your face was like what it never was afterwards, even in our happiest moments."

"We spoke of one thing and another, and while I held you close to me, clasped like a bunch of flowers, you told me about people we knew, you spoke of the sunlight that day and the coolness of the evening. But really you were telling me that you were mine. I felt your confession running through everything you said, and even if you did not express it, you actually gave me a confession of love.

"Ah, how great things are in the beginning! There is never any pettiness in the beginning.

"Once when we met in the public garden, I took you back at the end of the afternoon through the suburbs. The road was so peaceful and quiet that our footsteps seemed to disturb nature. Benumbed by emotion, we slackened our pace. I leaned over and kissed you."

"There," she said.

She put her finger on his neck.

"Gradually the kiss grew warmer. It crept toward your lips and stopped there. The first time it went astray, the second time it pretended it went astray. Soon I felt against my mouth"—he lowered his voice—"your mouth."

She bowed her head, and I saw her rosy mouth.

"It was all so beautiful in the midst of the watchfulness imprisoning me," she sighed, ever returning to her mild, pathetic preoccupation.

How she needed the stimulus of remembering her emotions, whether consciously or not! The recalling of these little dramas and former perils warmed her movements, renewed her love. That was the reason why she had had the whole story told her.

And he encouraged her. Their first enthusiasm returned, and now they tried to evoke the most exciting memories.

"It was sad, the day after you became mine, to see you again at a reception in your own home—inaccessible, surrounded by other people, mistress of a regular household, friendly to everybody, a bit timid, talking commonplaces. You bestowed the beauty of your face on everybody, myself included. But what was the use?

"You were wearing that cool-looking green dress, and they were teasing you about it. I did not dare to look at you when you passed me, and I thought of how happy we had been the day before."

"Ah," she sighed, as the beauty widened before her of all her memories, her thoughts, of all her soul, "love is not what they say it is. I, too, was stirred with anguish. How I had to conceal it, dissimulating every sign of my happiness, locking it hastily away within the coffer of my heart. At first I was afraid to go to sleep for fear of saying your name in a dream, and often, fighting against the stealthy invasion of sleep, I have leaned on my elbow, and remained with wide-open eyes, watching heroically over my heart.

"I was afraid of being recognised. I was afraid people would see the purity in which I was bathed. Yes, purity. When in the midst of life one wakes up from life, and sees a different brilliance in the daylight, and recreates everything, I call that purity.

"Do you remember the day we lost our way in the cab in Paris—the day he thought he recognised us from a distance, and jumped into another cab to follow us?"

She gave a start of ecstasy.

"Oh, yes," she murmured, "that was the great day!"

His voice quivered as if shaken by the throbbing of his heart, and his heart said:

"Kneeling on the seat, you looked out of the little window in the back of the cab and cried to me, 'He is nearer! He is further off! He will catch us. I do not see him any more. He has lost us.' Ah!"

And with one and the same movement their lips joined.

She breathed out like a sigh:

"That was the one time I enjoyed."

"We shall always be afraid," he said.

These words interlaced and changed into kisses. Their whole life surged into their lips.

Yes, they had to revive their past so as to love each other, they had constantly to be reassembling the pieces so as to keep their love from dying through staleness, as if they were undergoing, in darkness and in dust, in an icy ebbing away, the ruin of old age, the impress of death.

They clasped each other.

They were drowned in the darkness. They fell down, down into the shadows, into the abyss that they had willed.

He stammered:

"I will love you always."

But she and I both felt that he was lying again. We did not deceive ourselves. But what matter, what matter?

Her lips on his lips, she murmured like a thorny caress among the caresses:

"My husband will soon be home."

How little they really were at one! How, actually, there was nothing but their fear that they had in common, and how they stirred their fear up desperately. But their tremendous effort to commune somehow was soon to be over.

They stopped talking. Words had already accomplished the work of reviving their love. She merely murmured:

"I am yours, I am yours. I give myself to you. No, I do not give myself to you. How can I give myself when I do not belong to myself?"

"Are you happy?" she asked again.

"I swear you are everything in the world to me."

Now, she felt, their bliss had already become a mere memory, and she said almost plaintively:

"May God bless the bit of pleasure one has."

A doleful lament, the first signal of a tremendous fall, a prayer blasphemous yet divine.

I saw him look at the clock and at the door. He was thinking of leaving. He turned his face gently away from a kiss she was about to give him. There was a suggestion of uneasiness, almost disgust, in his expression.

"No," she said, "you are not going to love me always. You are going to leave me. But I regret nothing. I never will regret anything. Afterwards, when I return from—*this*—for good, to the great sorrow that will never leave me again, I shall say, 'I have had a lover,' and I shall come out from my nothingness to be happy for a moment."

He did not want to answer. He could not answer any more. He stammered:

"Why do you doubt me?"

But they turned their eyes toward the window. They were afraid, they were cold. They looked down at the space between the two houses and saw a vague remnant of twilight slip away like a ship of glory.

It seemed to me that the window beside them entered the scene. They gazed at it, dim, immense, blotting out everything around it. After the brief interval of sinful passion, they were overwhelmed as if, looking at the stainless azure of the window, they had seen a vision. Then their eyes met.

"See, we stay here," she said, "looking at each other like two miserable curs."

They separated. He seated himself on a chair, a sorry figure in the dusk.

His mouth was open, his face was contracted. His eyes and his jaw were self-condemnatory. You expected that in a few moments he would become emaciated, and you would see the eternal skeleton.

And at last both were alike in their setting, made so as much by their misery as by their human form. The night swallowed them up. I no longer saw them.

THEN, WHERE IS GOD, WHERE is God? Why does He not intervene in this frightful, regular crisis? Why does He not prevent, by a miracle, that fearful miracle by which one who is adored suddenly or gradually comes to be hated? Why does he not preserve man from having to mourn the loss of all his dreams? Why does he not preserve him from the distress of that sensuousness which flowers in his flesh and falls back on him again like spittle?

Perhaps because I am a man like the man in the room, like all other men, perhaps because what is bestial engrosses my attention now, I am utterly terrified by the invincible recoil of the flesh.

"It is everything in the world," he had said. "It is nothing," he had also said, but later. The echo of those two cries lingered in my ears. Those two cries, not shouted but uttered in a low scarcely audible voice, who shall declare their grandeur and the distance between them?

Who shall say? Above all, who shall know?

The man who can reply must be placed, as I am, above humanity, he must be both among and apart from human beings to see the smile turn into agony, the joy become satiety, and the union dissolve. For when you take full part in life you do not see this, you know nothing about it. You pass blindly from one extreme to the other. The man who uttered the two cries that I still hear, "Everything!" and "Nothing!" had forgotten the first when he was carried away by the second.

Who shall say? I wish some one would tell. What do words matter or conventions? Of what use is the time-honoured custom of writers of genius or mere talent to stop at the threshold of these descriptions, as if full descriptions were forbidden? The thing ought to be sung in a poem, in a masterpiece. It ought to be told down to the very bottom, if the purpose be to show the creative force of our hopes, of our wishes, which, when they burst into light, transform the world, overthrow reality.

What richer alms could you bestow on these two lovers, when again love will die between them? For this scene is not the last in their double story. They will begin again, like every human being. Once more they will try together, as much as they can, to seek shelter from life's defeats, to find ecstasy, to conquer death. Once more they will seek solace and deliverance. Again they will be seized by a thrill, by the force of sin, which clings to the flesh like a shred of flesh.

Yet once again, when once again they see that they put infinity into desire all in vain, they will be punished for the grandeur of their aspiration.

I do not regret having surprised this simple, terrible secret. Perhaps my having taken in and retained this sight in all its breadth, my having learned that the living truth is sadder and more sublime than I had ever believed, will be my sole glory.

VI

All was silent. They were gone. They had hidden elsewhere. The husband was coming. I gathered that from what they had said. But did I really know what they had said?

I paced up and down in my room, then dined, as in a dream, and went out, lured by humanity.

A cafe! The bright lighting beckoned to me to enter. Calm, simple, care-free people, who have no task like mine to accomplish.

Sitting by herself at a table, constantly looking around, was a girl with a painted face. A full glass was set in front of her and she held a little dog on her lap. His head reached over the edge of the marble table, and he comically sued on behalf of his mistress for the glances, even the smiles of the passersby.

The woman looked at me with interest. She saw I was not waiting for anybody or anything.

A sign, a word, and she, who was waiting for everybody, would come over to me with a smile. But no! I was simpler than that. If love troubled me, it was because of a great thought and not a mere instinct.

It was my misfortune to have a dream greater and stronger than I could bear.

Woe to those who dream of what they do not possess! They are right, but they are too right, and so are outside of nature. The simple, the weak, the humble pass carelessly by what is not meant for them. They touch everything lightly, without anguish. But the others! But I!

I wanted to take what was not mine. I wanted to steal. I wanted to live all lives, to dwell in all hearts.

Ah! I saw now how I should be punished for having entered into the living secrets of man. My punishment would fit my crime. I was destined to undergo the infinite misery I read in the others. I was to be punished by every mystery that kept its secret, by every woman who went by.

Infinity is not what we think. We associate it with heroes of legend and romance, and we invest fiery, exceptional characters, like a Hamlet, with infinity as with a theatrical costume. But infinity resides quietly in that man who is just passing by on the street. It resides in me, just as I am, with my ordinary face and name, in me, who want everything I have not. And there is no reason why there should be any limits to what I want.

So, step by step, I followed the track of the infinite. It made me suffer. Ah, if I did wrong, that great misery of mine, the tragedy of striving for the impossible, redeemed me. But I do not believe in redemption. I was suffering, and doubtless I looked like a martyr.

I had to go home to fulfil my martyrdom in the whole of its wretched duration. I had to go on looking. I was losing time in the world outside. I returned to my room, which welcomed me like a living being.

I PASSED TWO IDLE DAYS, watching fruitlessly.

I took to my hasty pacing to and fro again and succeeded, not without difficulty, in gaining a few days of respite, in making myself forget for a while.

I dwelt within these walls quiet in a feverish sort of way and inactive as a prisoner. I walked up and down my room a great part of the day, attracted by the opening in the wall and not daring to go away to a distance from it again.

The long hours went by, and in the evening I was worn out by my indefatigable hope.

THE ROOM WAS IN DISORDER. Amy was there with her husband. They had come back from a journey.

I had not heard them enter. I must have been too tired.

He had his hat on and was sitting on a chair beside the bed. She was dressing. I saw her disappear behind the washroom door. I looked at the husband. His features were regular and even seemed to show a certain nobility. The line of his forehead was clear cut. Only his mouth and moustache were somewhat coarse. He had a healthier, stronger appearance than her lover. His hand, which was toying with a cane, was fine, and there was a forceful elegance about his whole personality.

That was the man she hated and was deceiving. It was that head, that face, that expression which had lowered and disfigured themselves in her eyes, and were synonymous with her unhappiness.

All at once she was there in full view. My heart stood still and contracted and drew me toward her. She had nothing on but a short, thin chemise. She had come back a bit tired out by the thousands of little nothings she had already done. She had a toothbrush in her hand, her lips were moist and red, her hair dishevelled. Her legs were dainty, and the arch of her little feet was accentuated by her high-heeled shoes.

The air in the closed room was heavy with a mixture of odours—soap, face powder, the pungent scent of cologne.

She went out and came back again, warm and soapy, drying her face. This time she was all fresh and rosy.

He was talking about something, with his legs stretched out a little, sometimes looking at her, sometimes not looking at her.

"You know, the Bernards have not accepted."

He glanced at her, then looked down at the carpet and gave a disappointed cluck with his tongue, absorbed in this matter that interested him, while she kept going and coming, showing the lovely curves of her body.

She *was* lovely. But her husband went on droning his commonplaces, phrases that meant nothing to her, that were strange to her, and that seemed blasphemous in the room which held her beauty.

She put her garments on, one by one. Her husband continued in his bestial indifference, and dropped back into his reflections.

She went to the mirror over the mantelpiece with toilet articles spread out before her. Probably the mirror in the washroom was too small.

While keeping on with her toilet, she spoke as if to herself in a gay, animated, chatty way, because it was still the springtime of the day. She gave herself careful attention and took much time to groom herself. But this was an important matter, and the time was not lost. Besides, she was really hurrying.

Now she went to a wardrobe and took out a light dress of delicate texture, which she held out in her arms carefully.

She started to put the dress on, then an idea suddenly occurred to her and she stopped.

"No, no, no, decidedly not," she said.

She put the dress back and looked for another one, a dark skirt and a blouse.

She took a hat, fluffed the ribbon a bit, then held the trimming of roses close to her face in front of the mirror. Then she began to sing, evidently satisfied.

HE DID NOT LOOK AT her, and when he did look at her, he did not see her.

It was a solemn spectacle, a drama, but a drama dismal and depressing. That man was not happy, and yet I envied him his happiness.

　　　　　　　　　　　　　　　　　HENRI BARBUSSE

How explain this except by the fact that happiness is within us, within each of us, and is the desire for what we do not possess?

These two were together, but in reality far apart. They had left each other without leaving each other. A sort of intrigue about nothing held them together. They would never come nearer again, for between them lay the impassable barrier of love over and done with. This silence and this mutual ignorance are the cruelest things in the world. To cease to love is worse than to hate, for say what you will, death is worse than suffering.

I am sorry for the men and women who go through life together in the chains of indifference. I am sorry for the poor heart that has what it has for so short a time. I am sorry for the men who have the heart not to love any more.

And for a moment, seeing this simple harrowing scene, I underwent a little of the enormous suffering of those innumerable people who suffer all.

AMY FINISHED DRESSING. SHE PUT on a coat to match her skirt, leaving it partly open to show her transparent flesh-coloured lingerie waist. Then she left us—her husband and me.

He, too, made ready to leave, but the door opened again. Was it Amy coming back? No, it was the maid, who, seeing the room was occupied, started to withdraw.

"Excuse me, sir. I came to put the room in order, but I don't want to disturb you."

"You may stay."

She began to pick things up and close drawers. He raised his head and looked at her out of the corner of his eye. Then he rose and went over to her awkwardly, as though fascinated. A scuffling and an outcry, stifled by a coarse laugh. She dropped her brush and the gown she was holding. He caught her from behind and put his arms around her waist.

"Oh, go on! Stop! What-che doing?"

He did not say anything, but pressed her closer to him.

She laughed. Her hair came partly undone and fell down over her blowsy face. He trod on Amy's gown, which had dropped from the girl's hand. Then she felt the thing had gone far enough.

"Now, that'll do, that'll do," she said.

Since he still said nothing and brought his jaw close to her neck, she got angry.

"I told you, that'll do. Stop, I say. What's the matter with you?"

At length he let her go, and left, laughing a devilish laugh of shame and cynicism.

He went out, his passion still seething. But it was not only the overwhelming instinct that was stirring in him. A moment before that exquisite woman had unfolded herself in his presence in all her exquisite beauty, and he had not desired her.

Perhaps she denied herself to him. Perhaps they had an agreement with each other. But I plainly saw that even his eyes did not care, those same eyes which kindled at the sight of the servant girl, that ignoble Venus with untidy hair and dirty finger nails.

Because he did not know her, because she was different from the one whom he knew. To have what one has not. So, strange as it may seem, it was an idea, a lofty, eternal idea that guided his instinct.

I understood—I to whom it was given to behold these human crises—I understood that many things which we place outside ourselves are really inside ourselves, and that this was the secret.

How the veils drop off! How the intricacies unravel, and simplicity appears!

ONE DARK STORMY NIGHT TWO women came and occupied the Room. I could not see them and caught only fragments of their strange, whispered talk of love. From that time on the meals of the boarding-house had a magic attraction for me. I studied all the faces, trying to identify those two beings.

But I questioned pairs of faces in vain. I made efforts to detect resemblances. There was nothing to guide me. I knew them no more than if they had been buried in the dark night outside.

There were five girls or young women in the dining-room. One of them, at least, must have been an occupant of the Room that night. But a stronger will than mine shut off her countenance. I did not know, and I was overwhelmed by the nothingness of what I saw.

They left, one at a time. I did not know. My hands twitched in the infinity of uncertainty, and my fingers pressed the void. My face was there, my face, which was a definite thing, confronting everything possible, everything indefinite.

THE LADY THERE! I RECOGNISED Amy. She was talking to the landlady beside the window. I did not notice her at first, because of the other boarders between us.

HENRI BARBUSSE

She was eating grapes, daintily, with a rather studied manner.

I turned towards her. Her name was Madame Montgeron or Montgerot. It sounded funny to me. Why did she have that name? It seemed not to suit her, or to be useless. It struck me how artificial words and signs are.

The meal was over. Almost everybody had gone out. Coffee cups and sticky little liqueur glasses were scattered on the table on which a sunbeam shone, mottling the tablecloth and making the glasses sparkle. A coffee stain had dried on the cloth and gave out fragrance.

I joined in the conversation between Amy and Madame Lemercier. She looked at me. I scarcely recognised her look, which I had seen so clearly before.

The man-servant came in and whispered a few words to Madame Lemercier. She rose, excused herself, and went out of the room. I was left with Amy. There were only two or three people in the dining-room, who were discussing what they were going to do in the afternoon.

I did not know what to say to her. The conversation flagged and died out. She must have thought that she did not interest me—this woman, whose heart I had seen, and whose destiny I knew as well as God Himself.

She reached for a newspaper lying on the table, read a line or two, then folded it, rose and also left the room.

Sickened by the commonplaceness of life and dull from the heaviness of the after-lunch hour, I leaned drowsily on the long, long table, the sunlit table disappearing into infinity, and I made an effort to keep my arms from giving way, my chin from dropping, and my eyes from closing.

And in that disorderly room, where the servants were already hastening quietly to clear the table and make ready for the evening meal, I lingered almost alone, not knowing whether I was happy or unhappy, not knowing what was real and what was supernatural.

Then I understood. It came upon me softly, heavily. I looked around at all those simple, peaceful things. Then I closed my eyes, and said to myself, like a seer who gradually becomes conscious of the nature of the revelation he has seen, "The infinite—why, this is the infinite. It is true. I can no longer doubt." It came upon me with force that there is nothing strange on earth, that the supernatural does not exist, or, rather, that it is everywhere. It is in reality, in simplicity, in peace. It is here, inside these walls. The real and the supernatural are one and the same. There can no more be mystery in life than there can be a fourth dimension.

I, like other men, am moulded out of infinity. But how confused it all was to me! And I dreamed of myself, who could neither know myself well nor rid me of myself—myself who was like a deep shadow between my heart and the sun.

VII

The same background, the same half-light tarnishing them as when I first saw them together. Amy and her lover were seated beside each other, not far from me.

They seemed to have been talking for some time already.

She was sitting behind him, on the sofa, concealed by the shadow of the evening and the shadow of the man. He was bending over, pale and vaguely outlined, with his hands on his knees.

The night was still cloaked in the grey silken softness of evening. Soon it would cast off this mantle and appear in all its bare darkness. It was coming on them like an incurable illness. They seemed to have a presentiment of it and sought refuge from the fatal shadows in talking and thinking of other things.

They talked apathetically about this and that. I heard the names of places and people. They mentioned a railway station, a public walk, a florist.

All at once she stopped and hid her face in her hands.

He took her wrists, with a sad slowness that showed how much he was used to these spells, and spoke to her without knowing what to say, stammering and drawing as close as he could to her.

"Why are you crying? Tell me why you are crying."

She did not answer. Then she took her hands away from her eyes and looked at him.

"Why? Do I know? Tears are not words."

I watched her cry—drown herself in a flood of tears. It is a great thing to be in the presence of a rational being who cries. A weak, broken creature shedding tears makes the same impression as an all-powerful god to whom one prays. In her weakness and defeat Amy was above human power.

A kind of superstitious admiration seized me before this woman's face bathed from an inexhaustible source, this face sincere and truthful.

She stopped crying and lifted her head. Without his questioning her again she said:

"I am crying because one is alone.

"One cannot get away from one's self. One cannot even confess anything. One is alone. And then everything passes, everything changes, everything takes flight, and as soon as everything takes flight one is alone. There are times when I see this better than at other times. And then I cannot help crying."

She was getting sadder and sadder, but then she had a little access of pride, and I saw a smile gently stir her veil of melancholy.

"I am more sensitive than other people. Things that other people would not notice awaken a distinct echo in me, and in such moments of lucidity, when I look at myself, I see that I am alone, all alone, all alone."

Disturbed to see her growing distress, he tried to raise her spirits.

"We cannot say that, we who have reshaped our destiny. You, who have achieved a great act of will—"

But what he said was borne away like chaff.

"What good was it? Everything is useless. In spite of what I have tried to do, I am alone. My sin cannot change the face of things.

"It is not by sin that we attain happiness, nor is it by virtue, nor is it by that kind of divine fire by which one makes great instinctive decisions and which is neither good nor evil. It is by none of these things that one reaches happiness. One *never* reaches happiness."

She paused, and said, as if she felt her fate recoiling upon her:

"Yes, I know I have done wrong, that those who love me most would detest me if they knew. My mother, if she knew—she who is so indulgent—would be so unhappy. I know that our love exists with the reprobation of all that is wise and just and is condemned by my mother's tears. But what's the use of being ashamed any more? Mother, if you knew, you would have pity on my happiness."

"You are naughty," he murmured feebly.

She stroked the man's forehead lightly, and said in a tone of extraordinary assurance:

"You know I don't deserve to be called naughty. You know what I am saying is above a personal application. You know better than I do that one is alone. One day when I was speaking about the joy of living and you were as sad as I am today, you looked at me, and said you did not know what I was thinking, in spite of my explanations. You showed me that love is only a kind of festival of solitude, and holding me in your arms, you ended by exclaiming, 'Our love—I am our love,' and I gave the inevitable answer, alas, 'Our love—I am our love.'"

He wanted to speak, but she checked him.

"Stop! Take me, squeeze my hands, hold me close, give me a long, long kiss, do with me what you want—just to bring yourself close to me, close to me! And tell me that you are suffering. Why, don't you feel *my* grief?"

He said nothing, and in the twilight shroud that wrapped them round, I saw his head make the needless gesture of denial. I saw all the misery emanating from these two, who for once by chance in the shadows did not know how to lie any more.

It was true that they were there together, and yet there was nothing to unite them. There was a void between them. Say what you will, do what you will, revolt, break into a passion, dispute, threaten—in vain. Isolation will conquer you. I saw there was nothing to unite them, nothing.

She kept on in the same strain.

He seemed to be used to these sad monologues, uttered in the same tone, tremendous invocations to the impossible. He did not answer any more. He held her in his arms, rocked her quietly, and caressed her with delicate tenderness. He treated her as if she were a sick child he was nursing, without telling her what was the matter.

But he was disturbed by her contact. Even when prostrate and desolate, she quivered warm in his arms. He coveted this prey even though wounded. I saw his eyes fixed on her, while she gave herself up freely to her sadness. He pressed his body against hers. It was she whom he wanted. Her words he threw aside. He did not care for them. They did not caress him. It was she whom he wanted, she!

Separation! They were very much alike in ideas and temperament, and just then they were helping each other as much as they could. But I saw clearly—I who was a spectator apart from men and whose gaze soared above them—that they were strangers, and that in spite of all appearances they did not see nor hear each other any more. They conversed as best they could, but neither could yield to the other, and each tried to conquer the other. And this terrible battle broke my heart.

SHE UNDERSTOOD HIS DESIRE. SHE said plaintively, like a child at fault:

"I am not feeling well."

Then, in a sudden change of mood, she gave herself up to love, offering her whole self with her wounded woman's heart.

THEY ROSE AND SHOOK OFF the dream that had cast them to the ground.

He was as dejected as she. I bent over to catch what he was saying.

"If I had only known!" he breathed in a whisper.

Prostrated but more distrustful of each other with a crime between them, they went slowly over to the grey window, cleansed by a streak of twilight.

How much they were like themselves on the other evening. It *was* the other evening. Never had the impression been borne in upon me so strongly that actions are vain and pass like phantoms.

The man was seized with a trembling. And, vanquished, despoiled of all his pride, of all his masculine reserve, he no longer had the strength to keep back the avowal of shamed regret.

"One can't master one's self," he stammered, hanging his head. "It is fate."

They caught hold of each other's hands, shuddered slightly, panting, dispirited, tormented by their hearts.

Fate!

In so speaking they saw further than the flesh. In their remorse and disgust it was not mere physical disillusionment that so crushed them. They saw further. They were overcome by an impression of bleak truth, of aridity, of growing nothingness, at the thought that they had so many times grasped, rejected, and vainly grasped again their frail carnal ideal.

They felt that everything was fleeting, that everything wore out, that everything that was not dead would die, and that even the illusory ties holding them together would not endure. Their sadness did not bring them together. On the contrary, they were separated by all the force of their two sorrows. To suffer together, alas, what disunion!

And the condemnation of love itself came from her, in a cry of agony:

"Oh, our great, our immense love! I feel that little by little I am recovering from it!"

She threw back her head, and raised her eyes.

"Oh, the first time!" she said.

She went on, while both of them saw that first time when their hands had found each other.

"I knew that some day all that emotion would die, and, in spite of our promises, I wanted time to stand still.

"But time did not stand still, and now we scarcely love each other."

He made a gesture as of denial.

"It is not only you, my dear, who are drifting away," she continued. "I am, too. At first I thought it was only you. But then I understood my poor heart and realised that in spite of you, I could do nothing against time."

She went on slowly, now with her eyes turned away, now looking at him.

"Alas, some day, I may say to you, 'I no longer love you.' Alas, alas, some day I may say to you, 'I have never loved you!'

"This is the wound—time, which passes and changes us. The separation of human beings that deceive themselves is nothing in comparison. One can live even so. But the passage of time! To grow old, to think differently, to die. I am growing old and I am dying, I. It has taken me a long time to understand it. I am growing old. I *am* not old, but I am growing old. I have a few grey hairs already. The first grey hair, what a blow!

"Oh, this blotting out of the colour of your hair. It gives you the feeling of being covered with your shroud, of dry bones, and tombstones."

She rose and cried out into the void:

"Oh, to escape the network of wrinkles!"

"I said to myself, 'By slow degrees you will get there. Your skin will wither. Your eyes, which smile even in repose, will always be watering. Your breasts will shrink and hang on your skeleton like loose rags. Your lower jaw will sag from the tiredness of living. You will be in a constant shiver of cold, and your appearance will be cadaverous. Your voice will be cracked, and people who now find it charming to listen to you will be repelled. The dress that hides you too much now from men's eyes will not sufficiently hide your monstrous nudity, and people will turn their eyes away and not even dare to think of you.'"

She choked and put her hands to her mouth, overcome by the truth, as if she had too much to say. It was magnificent and terrifying.

He caught her in his arms, in dismay. But she was as in a delirium, transported by a universal grief. You would have thought that this funereal truth had just come to her like a sudden piece of bad news.

"I love you, but I love the past even more. I long for it, I long for it, I am consumed with longing for it. The past! I shall cry, I shall suffer because the past will never come back again.

"But love the past as much as you will, it will never come back. Death is everywhere, in the ugliness of what has been too long beautiful, in the tarnishing of what has been clean and pure, in the forgetfulness of what is long past, in daily habits, which are the forgetfulness of what is near. We catch only glimpses of life. Death is the one thing we really have time to see. Death is the only palpable thing. Of what use is it to be beautiful and chaste? They will walk over our graves just the same.

"A day is coming when I shall be no more. I am crying because I shall surely die. There is an invincible nothingness in everything and everybody. So when one thinks of that, dear, one smiles and forgives. One does not bear grudges. But goodness won in that way is worse than anything else."

HE BENT OVER AND KISSED her hands. He enveloped her in a warm, respectful silence, but, as always, I felt he was master of himself.

"I have always thought of death," she continued in a changed voice. "One day I confessed to my husband how it haunted me. He launched out furiously. He told me I was a neurasthenic and that he must look after me. He made me promise to be like himself and never think of such things, to be healthy and well-balanced, as he was.

"That was not true. It was he who suffered from the disease of tranquillity and indifference, a paralysis, a grey malady, and his blindness was an infirmity, and his peace was that of a dog who lives for the sake of living, of a beast with a human face.

"What was I to do? Pray? No. That eternal dialogue in which you are always alone is crushing. Throw yourself into some occupation? Work? No use. Doesn't work always have to be done over again? Have children and bring them up? That makes you feel both that you are done and finished and that you are beginning over again to no purpose. However, who knows?"

It was the first time that she softened.

"I have not been given the chance to practise the devotion, the submission, the humiliation of a mother. Perhaps that would have guided me in life. I was denied a little child."

For a moment, lowering her eyes, letting her hands fall, yielding to the maternal impulse, she only thought of loving and regretting the child that had not been vouchsafed to her—without perceiving that if she considered it her only possible salvation, it was because she did not have it.

"Charity? They say that it makes us forget everything. Oh, yes, to go distributing alms on the snowy streets, in a great fur cloak," she murmured and made a tired gesture, while the lover and I felt the shiver of the cold rainy evening and of all the winters past and yet to come.

"All that is diversion, deception. It does not alter the truth a particle. We shall die, we are going to die."

She stopped crying, dried her eyes and assumed a tone so positive and calm that it gave the impression that she was leaving the subject.

"I want to ask you a question. Answer me frankly. Have you ever dared, dear, even in the depths of your heart, to set a date, a date relatively far off, but exact and absolute, with four figures, and to say, 'No matter how old I shall live to be, on that day I shall be dead—while everything else will go on, and little by little my empty place will be destroyed or filled again?'"

The directness of her question disturbed him. But it seemed to me that he tried most to avoid giving her a reply that would heighten her obsession.

And all at once, she remembered something he had once said to her, and cleverly reminded him of it so as to close his mouth in advance and torture herself still more.

"Do you remember? One evening, by lamplight. I was looking through a book. You were watching me. You came to me, you knelt down and put your arms around my waist, and laid your head in my lap. There were tears in your eyes. I can still hear you. 'I am thinking,' you said, 'that this moment will never come again. I am thinking that you are going to change, to die, and go away. I am thinking so truly, so hotly, how precious these moments are, how precious you are, you who will never again be just what you are now, and I adore your ineffable presence as it is now.' You looked at my hand, you found it small and white, and you said it was an extraordinary treasure, which would disappear. Then you repeated, 'I adore you,' in a voice which trembled so, that I have never heard anything truer or more beautiful, for you were right as a god is right.

"Alas!" he said.

He saw the tears in her eyes. Then he bowed his head. When he lifted it again, I had a vague intuition that he would know what to answer, but had not yet formulated how to say it.

"Poor creatures, a brief existence, a few stray thoughts in the depths of a room—that is what we are," she said, lifting her head and looking at him, hoping for an impossible contradiction, as a child cries for a star.

He murmured:

"Who knows what we are?"

SHE INTERRUPTED HIM WITH A gesture of infinite weariness.

"I know what you are going to say. You are going to talk to me about the beauty of suffering. I know your noble ideas. I love them, my love, your beautiful theories, but I do not believe in them. I would believe them if they consoled me and effaced death."

With a manifest effort, as uncertain of himself as she was of herself, feeling his way, he replied:

"They would efface it, perhaps, if you believed in them."

She turned toward him and took one of his hands in both of hers. She questioned him with inexorable patience, then she slipped to her knees before him, like a lifeless body, humbled herself in the dust, wrecked in the depths of despair, and implored him:

"Oh, answer me! I should be so happy if you could answer me. I feel as though you really could!"

He bent over her, as if on the edge of an abyss of questioning: "Do you know what we are?" he murmured. "Everything we say, everything we think, everything we believe, is fictitious. We know nothing. Nothing is sure or solid."

"You are wrong," she cried. "There *is* something absolute, our sorrow, our need, our misery. We can see and touch it. Deny everything else, but our beggary, who can deny that?"

"You are right," he said, "it is the only absolute thing in the world."

"THEN, *WE* ARE THE ONLY absolute thing in the world," he deduced.

He caught at this. He had found a fulcrum. "We—" he said. He had found the cry against death, he repeated it, and tried again. "We—"

It was sublime to see him beginning to resist.

"It is we who endure forever."

"Endure forever! On the contrary, it is we who pass away."

"We see things pass, but we endure."

She shrugged her shoulders with an air of denial. There almost was hatred in her voice as she said:

"Yes—no—perhaps. After all, what difference does it make to me? That does not console me."

"Who knows—maybe we need sadness and shadow, to make joy and light."

"Light would exist without shadow," she insisted.

"No," he said gently.

"That does not console me," she said again.

THEN HE REMEMBERED THAT HE had already thought out all these things.

"Listen," he said, in a voice tremulous and rather solemn as if he were making a confession. "I once imagined two beings who were at the end of their life, and were recalling all they had suffered."

"A poem!" she said, discouraged.

"Yes," he said, "one of those which might be so beautiful."

It was remarkable to see how animated he became. For the first time he appeared sincere—when abandoning the living example of their own destiny for the fiction of his imagination. In referring to his poem, he had trembled. You felt he was becoming his genuine self and that he had faith. She raised her head to listen, moved by her tenacious need of hearing something, though she had no confidence in it.

"The man and the woman are believers," he began. "They are at the end of their life, and they are happy to die for the reasons that one is sad to live. They are a kind of Adam and Eve who dream of the paradise to which they are going to return. The paradise of purity. Paradise is light. Life on earth is obscurity. That is the motif of the song I have sketched, the light that they desire, the shadow that they are."

"Like us," said Amy.

He told of the life of the man and the woman of his poem. Amy listened to him, and accepted what he was saying. Once she put her hands on her heart and said, "Poor people!" Then she got a little excited. She felt he was going too far. She did not wish so much darkness, maybe because she was tired or because the picture when painted by some one else seemed exaggerated.

Dream and reality here coincided. The woman of the poem also protested at this point.

I was carried away by the poet's voice, as he recited, swaying slightly, in the spell of the harmony of his own dream:

"At the close of a life of pain and suffering the woman still looked ahead with the curiosity she had when she entered life. Eve ended as she had begun. All her subtle eager woman's soul climbed toward the secret as if it were a kind of kiss on the lips of her life. She wanted to be happy."

Amy was now more interested in her companion's words. The curse of the lovers in the poem, sister to the curse she felt upon herself, gave her confidence. But her personality seemed to be shrinking. A few moments before she had dominated everything. Now she was listening, waiting, absorbed.

"The lover reproached the woman for contradicting herself in claiming earthly and celestial happiness at the same time. She answered him with profundity, that the contradiction lay not in herself, but in the things she wanted.

"The lover then seized another healing wand and with desperate eagerness, he explained, he shouted, 'Divine happiness has not the same form as human happiness. Divine happiness is outside of ourselves.'

"The woman rose, trembling.

"'That is not true! That is not true!' she exclaimed. 'No, my happiness is not outside of me, seeing it is *my* happiness. The universe is God's universe, but I am the god of my own happiness. What I want,' she added, with perfect simplicity, 'is to be happy, I, just as I am, and with all my suffering.'"

Amy started. The woman in the poem had put her problem in a clearer and deeper manner, and Amy was more like that woman than herself.

"'I, with all my suffering,' the man repeated.

"Suffering—important word! It leads us to the heart of reality. Human suffering is a positive thing, which requires a positive answer, and sad as it is, the word is beautiful, because of the absolute truth it contains. 'I, with all my suffering!' It is an error to believe that we can be happy in perfect calm and clearness, as abstract as a formula. We are made too much out of shadow and some form of suffering. If everything that hurts us were to be removed, what would remain?

"And the woman said, 'My God, I do not wish for heaven!'"

"Well, then," said Amy, trembling, "it follows that we can be miserable in paradise."

"Paradise is life," said the poet.

Amy was silent and remained with her head lifted, comprehending at last that the whole poem was simply a reply to her question and that he had revived in her soul a loftier and a juster thought.

"Life is exalted to perfection as it ends," the poet went on. "'It is beautiful to reach the end of one's days,' said the lover. 'It is in this way that we have lived paradise.'

"There is the truth," the poet concluded. "It does not wipe out death. It does not diminish space, nor halt time. But it makes us what we are in essential. Happiness needs unhappiness. Joy goes hand in hand with sorrow. It is thanks to the shadow that we exist. We must not dream of an absurd abstraction. We must guard the bond that links us to blood and earth. 'Just as I am!' Remember that. We are a great mixture. We are more than we believe. Who knows what we are?"

On the woman's face, which the terror of death had rigidly contracted, a smile dawned. She asked with childish dignity:

"Why did you not tell me this right away when I asked you?"

"You would not have understood me then. You had run your dream of distress into a blind alley. I had to take the truth along a different way so as to present it to you anew."

AFTER THAT THEY FELL SILENT. For a fraction of time they had come as close to each other as human beings can come down here below—because of their august assent to the lofty truth, to the arduous truth (for it is hard to understand that happiness is at the same time happy and unhappy). She believed him, however, she, the rebel, she, the unbeliever, to whom he had given a true heart to touch.

VIII

The window was wide open. In the dusty rays of the sunset I saw three people with their backs to the long reddish-brown beams of light. An old man, with a care-worn, exhausted appearance and a face furrowed with wrinkles, seated in the armchair near the window. A tall young woman with very fair hair and the face of a madonna. And, a little apart, a woman who was pregnant.

She held her eyes fixed in front of her, seeming to contemplate the future. She did not enter into the conversation, perhaps because of her humbler condition, or because her thoughts were bent upon the event to come. The two others were conversing. The man had a cracked, uneven voice. A slight feverish tremour sometimes shook his shoulders, and now and then he gave a sudden involuntary jerk. The fire had died out of his eyes and his speech had traces of a foreign accent. The woman sat beside him quietly. She had the fairness and gentle calm of the northern races, so white and light that the daylight seemed to die more slowly than elsewhere upon her pale silver face and the abundant aureole of her hair.

Were they father and daughter or brother and sister? It was plain that he adored her but that she was not his wife.

With his dimmed eyes he looked at the reflection of the sunlight upon her.

"Some one is going to be born, and some one is going to die," he said.

The other woman started, while the man's companion cried in a low tone, bending over him quickly.

"Oh, Philip, don't say that."

He seemed indifferent to the effect he had produced, as though her protest had not been sincere, or else were in vain.

Perhaps, after all, he was not an old man. His hair seemed to me scarcely to have begun to turn grey. But he was in the grip of a mysterious illness, which he did not bear well. He was in a constant state of irritation. He had not long to live. That was apparent from unmistakable signs—the look of pity in the woman's eyes mingled with discreetly veiled alarm, and an oppressive atmosphere of mourning.

With a physical effort he began to speak so as to break the silence. As he was sitting between me and the open window, some of the things he said were lost in the air.

He spoke of his travels, and, I think, also of his marriage, but I did not hear well.

He became animated, and his voice rose painfully. He quivered. A restrained passion enlivened his gestures and glances and warmed his language. You could tell that he must have been an active brilliant man before his illness.

He turned his head a little and I could hear him better.

He told of the cities and countries that he had visited. It was like an invocation to sacred names, to far-off different skies, Italy, Egypt, India. He had come to this room to rest, between two stations, and he was resting uneasily, like an escaped convict. He said he would have to leave again, and his eyes sparkled. He spoke of what he still wanted to see. But the twilight deepened, the warmth left the air, and all he thought of now was what he had seen in the past.

"Think of everything we have seen, of all the space we bring with us."

They gave the impression of a group of travellers, never in repose, forever in flight, arrested for a moment in their insatiable course, in a corner of the world which you felt was made small by their presence.

"Palermo—Sicily."

Not daring to advance into the future, he intoxicated himself with these recollections. I saw the effort he was making to draw near to some luminous point in the days gone by.

"Carpi, Carpi," he cried. "Anna, do you remember that wonderful brilliant morning? The ferryman and his wife were at table in the open air. What a glow over the whole country! The table, round and pale like a star. The stream sparkling. The banks bordered with oleander and tamarisk. The sun made a flower of every leaf. The grass shone as if it were full of dew. The shrubs seemed bejewelled. The breeze was so faint that it was a smile, not a sigh."

She listened to him, placid, deep, and limpid as a mirror.

"The whole of the ferryman's family," he continued, "was not there. The young daughter was dreaming on a rustic seat, far enough away not to hear them. I saw the light-green shadow that the tree cast upon her, there at the edge of the forest's violet mystery.

"And I can still hear the flies buzzing in that Lombardy summer over the winding river which unfolded its charms as we walked along the banks."

"The greatest impression I ever had of noonday sunlight," he continued, "was in London, in a museum. An Italian boy in the dress of his country, a model, was standing in front of a picture which represented a sunlight effect on a Roman landscape. The boy held his head stretched out. Amid the immobility of the indifferent attendants, and in the dampness and drabness of a London day, this Italian boy radiated light. He was deaf to everything around him, full of secret sunlight, and his hands were almost clasped. He was praying to the divine picture."

"We saw Carpi again," said Anna. "We had to pass through it by chance in November. It was very cold. We wore all our furs, and the river was frozen."

"Yes, and we walked on the ice."

He paused for a moment, then asked:

"Why are certain memories imperishable?"

He buried his face in his nervous hands and sighed:

"Why, oh, why?"

"Our oasis," Anna said, to assist him in his memories, or perhaps because she shared in the intoxication of reviving them, "was the corner where the lindens and acacias were on your estate in the government of Kiev. One whole side of the lawn was always strewn with flowers in summer and leaves in winter."

"I can still see my father there," he said. "He had a kind face. He wore a great cloak of shaggy cloth, and a felt cap pulled down over his ears. He had a large white beard, and his eyes watered a little from the cold."

"Why," he wondered after a pause, "do I think of my father that way and no other way? I do not know, but that is the way he will live in me. That is the way he will not die."

THE DAY WAS DECLINING. THE woman seemed to stand out in greater relief against the other two and become more and more beautiful.

I saw the man's silhouette on the faded curtains, his back bent, his head shaking as in a palsy and his neck strained and emaciated.

With a rather awkward movement he drew a case of cigarettes from his pocket and lit a cigarette.

As the eager little light rose and spread like a glittering mask, I saw his ravaged features. But when he started to smoke in the twilight, all you could see was the glowing cigarette, shaken by an arm as unsubstantial as the smoke that came from it.

It was not tobacco that he was smoking. The odour of a drug sickened me.

He held out his hand feebly toward the closed window, modest with its half-lifted curtains.

"Look—Benares and Allahabad. A sumptuous ceremony—tiaras—insignia, and women's ornaments. In the foreground, the high priest, with his elaborate head-dress in tiers—a vague pagoda, architecture, epoch, race. How different we are from those creatures. Are *they* right or are *we* right?"

Now he extended the circle of the past, with a mighty effort.

"Our travels—all those bonds one leaves behind. All useless. Travelling does not make us greater. Why should the mere covering of ground make us greater?"

The man bowed his wasted head.

HE WHO HAD JUST BEEN in ecstasy now began to complain.

"I keep remembering—I keep remembering. My heart has no pity on me."

"Ah," he mourned, a moment afterwards, with a gesture of resignation, "we cannot say good-by to everything."

The woman was there, but she could do nothing, although so greatly adored. She was there with only her beauty. It was a superhuman vision that he evoked, heightened by regret, by remorse and greed. He did not want it to end. He wanted it back again. He loved his past.

Inexorable, motionless, the past is endowed with the attributes of divinity, because, for believers as well as for unbelievers, the great attribute of God is that of being prayed to.

THE PREGNANT WOMAN HAD GONE out. I saw her go to the door, softly with maternal carefulness of herself.

Anna and the sick man were left alone. The evening had a gripping reality. It seemed to live, to be firmly rooted, and to hold its place. Never before had the room been so full of it.

"One more day coming to an end," he said, and went on as if pursuing his train of thought:

"We must get everything ready for our marriage."

"Michel!" cried the young woman instinctively, as if she could not hold the name back.

"Michel will not be angry at us," the man replied. "He knows you love him, Anna. He will not be frightened by a formality, pure and simple—by a marriage *in extremis*," he added emphatically, smiling as though to console himself.

They looked at each other. He was dry, feverish. His words came from deep down in his being. She trembled.

With his eyes on her, so white and tall and radiant, he made a visible effort to hold himself in, as if not daring to reach her with a single word. Then he let himself go.

"I love you so much," he said simply.

"Ah," she answered, "you will not die!"

"How good you were," he replied, "to have been willing to be my sister for so long!"

"Think of all you have done for me!" she exclaimed, clasping her hands and bending her magnificent body toward him, as if prostrating herself before him.

You could tell that they were speaking open-heartedly. What a good thing it is to be frank and speak without reticence, without the shame and guilt of not knowing what one is saying and for each to go straight to the other. It is almost a miracle.

They were silent. He closed his eyes, though continuing to see her, then opened them again and looked at her.

"You are my angel who do not love me."

His face clouded. This simple sight overwhelmed me. It was the infiniteness of a heart partaking of nature—this clouding of his face.

I saw with what love he lifted himself up to her. She knew it. There was a great gentleness in her words, in her attitude toward him, which in every little detail showed that she knew his love. She did not encourage him, or lie to him, but whenever she could, by a word, by a gesture, or by some beautiful silence, she would try to console him a little for the harm she did him by her presence and by her absence.

After studying her face again, while the shadow drew him still nearer to her in spite of himself, he said:

"You are the sad confidante of my love of you."

He spoke of their marriage again. Since all preparations had been made, why not marry at once?

"My fortune, my name, Anna, the chaste love that will be left to you from me when—when I shall be gone."

He wanted to transform his caress—too light, alas—into a lasting benefit for the vague future. For the present all he aspired to was the feeble and fictitious union implied in the word marriage.

HENRI BARBUSSE

"Why speak of it?" she said, instead of giving a direct answer, feeling an almost insurmountable repugnance, doubtless because of her love for Michel, which the sick man had declared in her stead. While she had consented in principle to marrying him and had allowed the preliminary steps to be taken, she had never replied definitely to his urgings.

But it looked to me as if she were about to make a different decision, one contrary to her material interests, in all the purity of her soul, which was so transparent—the decision to give herself to him freely.

"Tell me!" he murmured.

There was almost a smile on her mouth, the mouth to which supplications had been offered as to an altar.

The dying man, feeling that she was about to accept, murmured:

"I love life." He shook his head. "I have so little time left, so little time that I do not want to sleep at night any more."

Then he paused and waited for her to speak.

"Yes," she said, and lightly touched—hardly grazed—the old man's hand with her own.

And in spite of myself, my inexorable, attentive eye could not help detecting the stamp of theatrical solemnity, of conscious grandeur in her gesture. Even though devoted and chaste, without any ulterior motive, her sacrifice had a self-glorifying pride, which I perceived—I who saw everything.

In the boarding-house, the strangers were the sole topic of conversation. They occupied three rooms and had a great deal of baggage, and the man seemed to be very rich, though simple in his tastes. They were to stay in Paris until the young woman's delivery, in a month or so. She expected to go to a hospital nearby. But the man was very ill, they said. Madame Lemercier was extremely annoyed. She was afraid he would die in her house. She had made arrangements by correspondence, otherwise she would not have taken these people in—in spite of the tone that their wealth might give to her house. She hoped he would last long enough to be able to leave. But when you spoke to her, she seemed to be worried.

When I saw him again, I felt he was really going to die soon. He sat in his chair, collapsed, with his elbows on the arms of the chair and his hands drooping. It seemed difficult for him to look at things, and he held his face bowed down, so that the light from the window did not reveal his pupils, but only the edge of the lower lids, which gave the impression of his eyes having been put out. I remembered what the poet had said, and I trembled before this man whose life was over, who reviewed almost his entire existence like a terrible sovereign, and was wrapped in a beauty that was of God.

IX

S ome one knocked at the door.

It was time for the doctor. The sick man raised himself uncertainly in awe of the master.

"How have you been today?"

"Bad."

"Well, well," the doctor said lightly.

They were left alone together. The man dropped down again with a slowness and awkwardness that would have seemed ridiculous if it had not been so sad. The doctor stood between us.

"How has your heart been behaving?"

By an instinct which seemed tragic to me, they both lowered their voices, and in a low tone the sick man gave his daily account of the progress of his malady.

The man of science listened, interrupted, and nodded his head in approval. He put an end to the recital by repeating his usual meaningless assurances, in a raised voice now and with his usual broad gesture.

"Well, well, I see there's nothing new."

He shifted his position and I saw the patient, his drawn features and wild eyes. He was all shaken up by this talking about the dreadful riddle of his illness.

He calmed himself, and began to converse with the doctor, who let himself down squarely into a chair, with an affable manner. He started several topics, then in spite of himself returned to the sinister thing he carried within him, his disease.

"Disgusting!" he said.

"Bah!" said the doctor, who was blasé.

Then he rose.

"Well, till tomorrow!"

"Yes, for the consultation."

"Yes. Well, good-by!"

The doctor went out, lightly carrying the burden of misery and cruel memories, the weight of which he had ceased to feel.

EVIDENTLY THE CONSULTING PHYSICIANS HAD just finished their examination of the patient in another room. The door opened, and two doctors entered.

Their manner seemed to me to be stiff. One of them was a young man, the other an old man.

They looked at each other. I tried to penetrate the silence of their eyes and the night in their heads. The older man stroked his beard, leaned against the mantelpiece, and stared at the ground.

"Hopeless," he said, lowering his voice, for fear of being overheard by the patient.

The other nodded his head—in sign of agreement—of complicity, you might say. Both men fell silent like two guilty children. Their eyes met again.

"How old is he?"

"Fifty-three."

"Lucky to live so long," the young doctor remarked.

To which the old man retorted philosophically:

"Yes, indeed. But his luck won't hold out any longer."

A silence. The man with the grey beard murmured:

"I detected sarcoma." He put his finger on his neck. "Right here."

The other man nodded—his head seemed to be nodding continually—and muttered:

"Yes. There's no possibility of operating."

"Of course not," said the old specialist, his eyes shining with a kind of sinister irony. "There's only one thing that could remove it—the guillotine. Besides, the malignant condition has spread. There is pressure upon the submaxillary and subclavicular ganglia, and probably the axillary ganglia also. His respiration, circulation and digestion will soon be obstructed and strangulation will be rapid."

He sighed and stood with an unlighted cigar in his mouth, his face rigid, his arms folded. The young man sat down, leaning back in his chair, and tapped the marble mantelpiece with his idle fingers.

"What shall I tell the young woman?"

"Put on a subdued manner and tell her it is serious, very serious, but no one can tell, nature is infinitely resourceful."

"That's so hackneyed."

"So much the better," said the old man.

"But if she insists on knowing?"

"Don't give in."

"Shall we not hold out a little hope? She is so young."

"No. For that very reason we mustn't. She'd become too hopeful. My boy, never say anything superfluous at such a time. There's no use. The only result is to make them call us ignoramuses and hate us."

"Does he realise?"

"I do not know. While I examined him—you heard—I tried to find out by asking questions. Once I thought he had no suspicion at all. Then he seemed to understand his case as well as I did."

"Sarcoma forms like the human embryo," said the younger doctor.

"Yes, like the human embryo," the other assented and entered into a long elaboration of this idea.

"The germ acts on the cell, as Lancereaux has pointed out, in the same way as a spermatozoon. It is a micro-organism which penetrates the tissue, and selects and impregnates it, sets it vibrating, gives it *another life*. But the exciting agent of this intracellular activity, instead of being the normal germ of life, is a parasite."

He went on to describe the process minutely and in highly scientific terms, and ended up by saying:

"The cancerous tissue never achieves full development. It keeps on without ever reaching a limit. Yes, cancer, in the strictest sense of the word, is infinite in our organism."

The young doctor bowed assent, and then said:

"Perhaps—no doubt—we shall succeed in time in curing all diseases. Everything can change. We shall find the proper method for preventing what we cannot stop when it has once begun. And it is then only that we shall dare to tell the ravages due to the spread of incurable diseases. Perhaps we shall even succeed in finding cures for certain incurable affections. The remedies have not had time to prove themselves. We shall cure others—that is certain—but we shall not cure him." His voice deepened. Then he asked:

"Is he a Russian or a Greek?"

"I do not know. I see so much into the inside of people that their outsides all look alike to me."

"They are especially alike in their vile pretense of being dissimilar and enemies."

The young man seemed to shudder, as if the idea aroused a kind of passion in him. He rose, full of anger, changed.

"Oh," he said, "what a disgraceful spectacle humanity presents. In spite of its fearful wounds, humanity makes war upon humanity. We who deal with the sores afflicting mankind are struck more than others by all the evil men involuntarily inflict upon one another. I am neither a politician nor a propagandist. It is not my business to occupy myself with ideas. I have too much else to do. But sometimes I am moved by a great pity, as lofty as a dream. Sometimes I feel like punishing men, at other times, like going down on my knees to them."

The old doctor smiled sadly at this vehemence, then his smile vanished at the thought of the undeniable outrage.

"Unfortunately you are right. With all the misery we have to suffer, we tear ourselves with our own hands besides—the war of the classes, the war of the nations, whether you look at us from afar or from above, we are barbarians and madmen."

"Why, why," said the young doctor, who was getting excited, "why do we continue to be fools when we recognise our own folly?"

The old practitioner shrugged his shoulders, as he had a few moments before when they spoke of incurable diseases.

"The force of tradition, fanned by interested parties. We are not free, we are attached to the past. We study what has always been done, and do it over again—war and injustice. Some day perhaps humanity will succeed in ridding itself of the ghost of the past. Let us hope that some day we shall emerge from this endless epoch of massacre and misery. What else is there to do than to hope?"

The old man stopped at this. The young man said:

"To will."

The other man made a gesture with his hand.

"There is one great general cause for the world's ulcer," the younger one kept on. "You have said it—servility to the past, prejudice which prevents us from doing things differently, according to reason and morality. The spirit of tradition infects humanity, and its two frightful manifestations are—"

The old man rose from his chair, as if about to protest and as if to say, "Don't mention them!"

But the young man could not restrain himself any more.

"—inheritance from the past and the fatherland."

"Hush!" cried the old man. "You are treading on ground on which I cannot follow. I recognise present evils. I pray with all my heart for the new era. More than that, I believe in it. But do not speak that way about two sacred principles."

"You speak like everybody else," said the young man bitterly. "We must go to the root of the evil, you know we must. *You* certainly do." And he added violently, "Why do you act as if you did not know it? If we wish to cure ourselves of oppression and war, we have a right to attack them by all the means possible—all!—the principle of inheritance and the cult of the fatherland."

"No, we haven't the right," exclaimed the old man, who had risen in great agitation and threw a look at his interlocutor that was hard, almost savage.

"We have the right!" cried the other.

All at once, the grey head drooped, and the old man said in a low voice:

"Yes, it is true, we have the right. I remember one day during the war. We were standing beside a dying man. No one knew who he was. He had been found in the debris of a bombarded ambulance—whether bombarded purposely or not, the result was the same. His face had been mutilated beyond recognition. All you could tell was that he belonged to one or other of the two armies. He moaned and groaned and sobbed and shrieked and invented the most appalling cries. We listened to the sounds that he made in his agony, trying to find one word, the faintest accent, that would at least indicate his nationality. No use. Not a single intelligible sound from that something like a face quivering on the stretcher. We looked and listened, until he fell silent. When he was dead and we stopped trembling, I had a flash of comprehension. I understood. I understood in the depths of my being that man is more closely knit to man than to his vague compatriots.

"Yes, we have a right to attack oppression and war, we have a right to. I saw the truth several times afterward again, but I am an old man, and I haven't the strength to stick to it."

"My dear sir," said the young man, rising, with respect in his voice. Evidently he was touched.

"Yes, I know, I know," the old scientist continued in an outburst of sincerity. "I know that in spite of all the arguments and the maze of special cases in which people lose themselves, the absolute, simple truth remains, that the law by which some are born rich and others poor and which maintains a chronic inequality in society is a supreme injustice. It rests on no better basis than the law that once created races of slaves. I know patriotism has become a narrow offensive sentiment which as long as it lives will maintain war and exhaust the world. I know that neither work nor material and moral prosperity, nor the noble refinements of progress, nor the wonders of art, need competition inspired by hate. In fact, I know that, on the contrary, these things are destroyed by arms.

I know that the map of a country is composed of conventional lines and different names, that our innate love of self leads us closer to those that are like-minded than to those who belong to the same geographical group, and we are more truly compatriots of those who understand and love us and who are on the level of our own souls, or who suffer the same slavery than of those whom we meet on the street. The national groups, the units of the modern world, are what they are, to be sure. The love we have for our native land would be good and praiseworthy if it did not degenerate, as we see it does everywhere, into vanity, the spirit of predominance, acquisitiveness, hate, envy, nationalism, and militarism. The monstrous distortion of the patriotic sentiment, which is increasing, is killing off humanity. Mankind is committing suicide, and our age is an agony."

The two men had the same vision and said simultaneously:

"A cancer, a cancer!"

The older scientist grew animated, succumbing to the evidence.

"I know as well as you do that posterity will judge severely those who have made a fetich of the institutions of oppression and have cultivated and spread the ideas supporting them. I know that the cure for an abuse does not begin until we refuse to submit to the cult that consecrates it. And I, who have devoted myself for half a century to the great discoveries that have changed the face of the world, I know that in introducing an innovation one encounters the hostility of everything that is.

"I know it is a vice to spend years and centuries saying of progress, 'I should like it, but I do not want it.' But as for me, I have too many cares and too much work to do. And then, as I told you, I am too old. These ideas are too new for me. A man's intelligence is capable of holding only a certain quantum of new, creative ideas. When that amount is exhausted, whatever the progress around you may be, one refuses to see it and help it on. I am incapable of carrying on a discussion to fruitful lengths. I am incapable of the audacity of being logical. I confess to you, my boy, I have not the strength to be right."

"My dear doctor," said the young man in a tone of reproach, meeting his older colleague's sincerity with equal sincerity, "you have publicly declared your disapproval of the men who publicly fought the idea of patriotism. The influence of your name has been used against them."

The old man straightened himself, and his face coloured.

"I will not stand for our country's being endangered."

I did not recognise him any more. He dropped from his great thoughts and was no longer himself. I was discouraged.

"But," the other put in, "what you just said—"

"That is not the same thing. The people you speak of have defied us. They have declared themselves enemies and so have justified all outrages in advance."

"Those who commit outrages against them commit the crime of ignorance," said the young man in a tremulous voice, sustained by a kind of vision. "They fail to see the superior logic of things that are in the process of creation." He bent over to his companion, and, in a firmer tone, asked, "How can the thing that is beginning help being revolutionary? Those who are the first to cry out are alone, and therefore ignored or despised. You yourself just said so. But posterity will remember the vanguard of martyrs. It will hail those who have cast a doubt on the equivocal word 'fatherland,' and will gather them into the fold of all the innovators who went before them and who are now universally honoured."

"Never!" cried the old man, who listened to this last with a troubled look. A frown of obstinacy and impatience deepened in his forehead, and he clenched his fists in hate. "No, that is not the same thing. Besides, discussions like this lead nowhere. It would be better, while we are waiting for the world to do its duty, for us to do ours and tell this poor woman the truth."

X

The two women were alone beside the wide open window. In the full, wise light of the autumn sun, I saw how faded was the face of the pregnant woman.

All of a sudden a frightened expression came into her eyes. She reeled against the wall, leaned there a second, and then fell over with a stifled cry.

Anna caught her in her arms, and dragged her along until she reached the bell and rang and rang. Then she stood still, not daring to budge, holding in her arms the heavy delicate woman, her own face close to the face with the rolling eyes. The cries, dull and stifled at first, burst out now in loud shrieks.

The door opened. People hurried in. Outside the door the servants were on the watch. I caught sight of the landlady, who succeeded ill in concealing her comic chagrin.

They laid the woman on the bed. They removed ornaments, unfolded towels, and gave hurried orders.

The crisis subsided and the woman stopped shrieking. She was so happy not to be suffering any more that she laughed. A somewhat constrained reflection of her laugh appeared on the faces bending over her. They undressed her carefully. She let them handle her like a child. They fixed the bed. Her legs looked very thin and her set face seemed reduced to nothing. All you saw was her distended body in the middle of the bed. Her hair was undone and spread around her face like a pool. Two feminine hands plaited it quickly.

Her laughter broke and stopped.

"It is beginning again."

A groan, which grew louder, a fresh burst of shrieks. Anna, her only friend, remained in the room. She looked and listened, filled with thoughts of motherhood. She was thinking that she, too, held within her such travail and such cries.

This lasted the whole day. For hours, from morning until evening, I heard the heart-rending wail rising and falling from that pitiful double being.

At certain moments I fell back, overcome. I could no longer look or listen. I renounced seeing so much truth. Then once more, with an effort, I stood up against the wall and looked into the Room again.

HENRI BARBUSSE

Anna kissed the woman on her forehead, in brave proximity to the immense cry.

When the cry was articulate, it was: "No, no! I do not want to!"

Serious, sickened faces, almost grown old in a few hours with fatigue, passed and repassed.

I heard some one say:

"No need to help it along. Nature must be allowed to take her course. Whatever nature does she does well."

And in surprise my lips repeated this lie, while my eyes were fixed upon the frail, innocent woman who was a prey to stupendous nature, which crushed her, rolled her in her blood, and exacted all the suffering from her that she could yield.

The midwife turned up her sleeves and put on her rubber gloves. She waved her enormous reddish-black, glistening hands like Indian clubs.

And all this turned into a nightmare in which I half believed. My head grew heavy and I was sickened by the smell of blood and carbolic acid poured out by the bottleful.

At a moment when I, feeling too harrowed, was not looking, I heard a cry different from hers, a cry that was scarcely more than the sound of a moving object, a light grating. It was the new being that had unloosened itself, as yet a mere morsel of flesh taken from her flesh—her heart which had just been torn away from her.

This shook me to the depths of my being. I, who had witnessed everything that human beings undergo, I, at this first signal of human life, felt some paternal and fraternal chord—I do not know what—vibrating within me.

She laughed. "How quickly it went!" she said.

THE DAY WAS COMING TO a close. Complete silence in the room. A plain night lamp was burning, the flame scarcely flickering. The clock, like a poor soul, was ticking faintly. There was hardly a thing near the bed. It was as in a real temple.

She lay stretched out in bed, in ideal quiet, her eyes turned toward the window. Bit by bit, she saw the evening descending upon the most beautiful day in her life.

This ruined mass, this languid face shone with the glory of having created, with a sort of ecstasy which redeemed her suffering, and one saw the new world of thoughts that grew out of her experience.

She thought of the child growing up. She smiled at the joys and sorrows it would cause her. She smiled also at the brother or sister it would have some day.

And I thought of this at the same time that she did, and I saw her martyrdom more clearly than she.

This massacre, this tragedy of flesh is so ordinary and commonplace that every woman carries the memory and imprint of it, and yet nobody really knows it. The doctor, who comes into contact with so much of the same sort of suffering, is not moved by it any more. The woman, who is too tender-hearted, never remembers it. Others who look on at travail have a sentimental interest, which wipes out the agony. But I who saw for the sake of seeing know, in all its horror, the agony of childbirth. I shall never forget the great laceration of life.

The night lamp was placed so that the bed was plunged in shadow. I could no longer see the mother. I no longer knew her. I believed in her.

XI

The woman who had been confined was moved with exquisite care into the next room, which she had occupied previously. It was larger and more comfortable.

They cleaned the room from top to bottom, and I saw Anna and Philip seated in the room again.

"Take care, Philip," Anna was saying, "you do not understand the Christian religion. You really do not know *exactly* what it is. You speak of it," she added, with a smile, "as women speak of men, or as men when they try to explain women. Its fundamental element is love. It is a covenant of love between human beings who instinctively detest one another. It is also a wealth of love in our hearts to which we respond naturally when we are little children. Later all our tenderness is added to it bit by bit, like treasure to treasure. It is a law of outpouring to which we give ourselves up, and it is the source of that outpouring. It is life, it is almost a work, it is almost a human being."

"But, my dear Anna, that is not the Christian religion. That is you."

IN THE MIDDLE OF THE night, I heard talking through the partition. I struggled with my sleepiness and got up.

The man was alone, in bed. A lamp was burning dimly. He was asleep and talking in his sleep.

He smiled and said "No!" three times with growing ecstasy. Then his smile at the vision he saw faded away. For a moment his face remained set, as if he were waiting, then he looked terrified, and his mouth opened. "Anna! Ah, ah!—Ah, ah!" he cried through gaping lips. At this he awoke and rolled his eyes. He sighed and quieted down. He sat up in bed, still struck and terrified by what had passed through his mind a few seconds before.

He looked round at everything to calm himself and banish his nightmare completely. The familiar sight of the room, with the lamp, so wise and motionless, enthroned in the middle, reassured him. It was balm to this man who had just seen what does not exist, who had just smiled at phantoms and touched them, who had just been mad.

I ROSE THE NEXT MORNING, all broken up. I was restless. I had a severe headache. My eyes were bloodshot. When I looked at them in the mirror, it was as if I saw them through a veil of blood.

When I was alone, free from the visions and scenes to which I devoted my life, all kinds of worries assailed me—worry about my position, which I was risking, worry about the steps I ought to be taking and yet was not taking, worry over myself that I was so intent upon casting off all my obligations and postponing them, and repudiating my wage-earning lot, by which I was destined to be held fast in the slow wheelwork of office routine.

I was also worried by all kinds of minutiæ, annoying because they kept cropping up every minute—not make any noise, not light a light when the Room was dark, hide myself, and hide myself all the time. One evening I got a fit of coughing while listening at the hole. I snatched up my pillow and buried my head in it to keep the sound from coming out of my mouth.

Everything seemed to be in a league to avenge itself upon me for I did not know what. I felt as though I should not be able to hold out much longer. Nevertheless, I made up my mind to keep on looking as long as my health and my courage lasted. It might be bad for me, but it was my duty.

THE MAN WAS SINKING. DEATH was evidently in the house.

It was quite late in the evening. They were sitting at the table opposite each other.

I knew their marriage had taken place that afternoon, and that its purpose had been only to solemnise their approaching farewell. Some white blossoms, lilies and azaleas, were strewn on the table, the mantelpiece, and one armchair. He was fading away like those cut flowers.

"We are married," he said. "You are my wife. You are my wife, Anna!"

It was for the sweetness of saying, "You are my wife," that he had so longed. Nothing more. But he felt so poor, with his few days of life, that it was complete happiness to him.

He looked at her, and she lifted her eyes to him—to him who adored her sisterly tenderness—she who had become devoted to his adoration. What infinite emotion lay hidden in these two silences, which faced each other in a kind of embrace; in the double silence of these two human beings, who, I had observed, never touched each other, not even with the tips of their fingers.

The girl lifted her head, and said, in an unsteady voice:

"It is late. I am going to sleep."

She got up. The lamp, which she set on the mantelpiece, lit up the room.

She trembled. She seemed to be in a dream and not to know how to yield to the dream. Then she raised her arm and took the pins out of her hair. It fell down her back and looked, in the night, as if it were lit by the setting sun.

The man made a sudden movement and looked at her in surprise. Not a word.

She removed a gold brooch from the top of her blouse, and a bit of her bosom appeared.

"What are you doing, Anna, what are you doing?"

"Why, undressing."

She wanted to say this in a natural voice, but had not succeeded. He replied with an inarticulate exclamation, a cry from his heart, which was touched to the quick. Stupefaction, desperate regret, and also the flash of an inconceivable hope agitated him, oppressed him.

"You are my husband."

"Oh," he said, "you know I am nothing." He spoke feebly in a tragic tone. "Married for form's sake," he went on, stammering out fragmentary, incoherent phrases. "I knew it, I knew it—formality—our conventions—"

She stopped, with her hand hesitating on her blouse like a flower, and said:

"You are my husband. It is your right."

He made a faint gesture of denial. She quickly corrected herself.

"No, no, it is not your right. I want to do it."

I began to understand how kind she was trying to be. She wished to give this man, this poor man who was sinking at her feet, a reward that was worthy of her. She wanted to bestow upon him the gift of the sight of her body.

But the thing was harder than the mere bestowal of a gift. It must not look like the mere payment of a debt. He would not have consented to that. She must make him believe it was a voluntary wifely act, a willing caress. She must conceal her suffering and repugnance like a vice. Feeling the difficulty of giving this delicate shade to her sacrifice, she was afraid of herself.

"No, Anna—dear Anna—think—" He was going to say, "Think of Michel," but he did not have the strength at that moment to use this one decisive argument, and only murmured, "You, you!"

"I want to do it," she repeated.

"But I do not want you to. No, no."

He said this in a weaker voice now, overcome by love. Through instinctive nobility, he covered his eyes with his hand, but gradually his hand surrendered and dropped.

She continued to undress, with uncertain movements that showed she hardly knew what she was doing. She took off her black waist, and her bust emerged like the day. When the light shone on her she quivered and crossed her shining arms over her chest. Then she started to unhook the belt of her skirt, her arms curved, her reddened face bent down and her lips tightly compressed, as if she had nothing in mind but the unhooking of her skirt. It dropped to the ground and she stepped out of it with a soft rustle, like the sound the wind makes in a leafy garden.

She leaned against the mantelpiece. Her movements were large, majestic, beautiful, yet dainty and feminine. She pulled off her stockings. Her legs were round and large and smooth as in a statue of Michael Angelo's.

She shivered and stopped, overcome by repugnance.

"I feel a little cold," she said in explanation and went on undressing, revealing her great modesty in violating it.

"Holy Virgin!" the man breathed in a whisper, so as not to frighten her.

I HAVE NEVER SEEN A woman so radiantly beautiful. I had never dreamed of beauty like it. The very first day, her face had struck me by its regularity and unusual charm, and her tall figure—taller than myself—had seemed opulent, yet delicate, but I had never believed in such splendid perfection of form.

In her superhuman proportions she was like some Eve in grand religious frescoes. Big, soft and supple, broad-shouldered, with a full beautiful bosom, small feet, and tapering limbs.

In a dreamy voice, going still further in the bestowal of her supreme gift, she said:

"No one"—she stressed these words with an emphasis amounting to the mention of a certain name—"*no one*—listen—no one, no matter what happens, will ever know what I have just done."

And now she, the giver of a gift, knelt—knelt to her adorer who was prostrated before her like a victim. Her shining knees touched the cheap common carpet. Her chastity clothed her like a beautiful garment. She murmured broken words of gratitude, as though she felt that what she was doing was higher than her duty and more beautiful, and that it glorified her.

AFTER SHE DRESSED AND LEFT the room without their having dared to say anything to each other, I wavered between two doubts. Was she right, or was she wrong? I saw the man cry and I heard him mutter:

"Now I shall not be able to die."

XII

The man was lying in bed. They moved about him carefully. He stirred faintly, said a few words, asked for a drink, smiled and then became silent under the rush of thoughts.

That morning they had seen him fold his hands, and they had asked him whether he wanted them to send for a priest.

"Yes—no," he said.

They went out, and a few minutes later, as if he had been waiting outside the door, a dark-robed priest entered. The two were left alone together.

The dying man turned his face toward the newcomer.

"I am going to die," he said.

"What is your religion?" asked the priest.

"The religion of my own country, the Greek Orthodox Church."

"That is a heresy which you must instantly abjure. There is only one true religion, the Roman Catholic religion. Confess now. I will absolve you and baptise you."

The other did not reply.

"Tell me what sins you have committed. You will repent and everything will be forgiven you."

"My sins?"

"Try to remember. Shall I help you?" He nodded toward the door. "Who is that person?"

"My—wife," said the man with slight hesitation, which did not escape the priest, who was leaning over him with ears pricked. He smelt a rat.

"How long has she been your wife?"

"Two days."

"Oh, two days! Now I have struck it. And before that, you sinned with her?"

"No," said the man.

The priest was put out of countenance.

"Well, I suppose you are not lying. Why didn't you sin? It is unnatural. After all," he insisted, "you are a man."

The sick man was bewildered and began to get excited. Seeing this, the priest said:

"Do not be surprised, my son, if my questions are direct and to the point. I ask you in all simplicity, as is my august duty as a priest. Answer

HENRI BARBUSSE

me in the same simple spirit, and you will enter into communion with God," he added, not without kindness.

"She is a young girl," said the old man. "I took her under my protection when she was quite a child. She shared the hardships of my traveller's life, and took care of me. I married her before my death because I am rich and she is poor."

"Was that the only reason—no other reason at all?"

He fixed his look searchingly on the dying man's face, then said, "Eh?" smiling and winking an eye, almost like an accomplice.

"I love her," said the man.

"At last, you are confessing!" cried the priest. He buried his eyes in the eyes of the dying man. The things he said fairly hit him as he lay there.

"So you desired this woman, the flesh of this woman, and for a long time committed a sin in spirit? Didn't you? Eh?

"Tell me, when you were travelling together, how did you arrange for rooms and beds in the hotels?

"You say she took care of you? What did she have to do for you?"

The two men scanned each other's faces keenly, and I saw the misunderstanding between them growing.

The dying man withdrew into himself and became hardened, incredulous before this stranger, with the vulgar appearance, in whose mouth the words of God and truth assumed a grotesque aspect.

However, he made an effort:

"If I have sinned in spirit, to use your words," he said, "it proves that I have not sinned in reality, and why should I repent of what was suffering pure and simple?"

"No theories now. We are not here for theorising. I tell you, a sin committed in spirit is committed in intention, and therefore in effect, and must be confessed and redeemed. Tell me how often you succumbed to guilty thoughts. Give me details."

"But I resisted," moaned the unfortunate man. "That is all I have to say."

"That is not enough. The stain—you are now convinced, I presume, of the justice of the term—the stain ought to be washed out by the truth."

"Very well," said the dying man. "I confess I have committed the sin, and I repent of it."

"That is not a confession, and is none of my business," retorted the priest. "Now tell me, under exactly what circumstances did you yield to temptation with that person, to the suggestions of the evil spirit?"

The man was swept by a wave of rebellion. He half rose and leaned on his elbow, glaring at the stranger, who returned his look steadily.

"Why have I the evil spirit in me?" he demanded.

"You are not the only one. All men have it."

"Then it is God who put it into them, since it is God who made them."

"Ah, you are a debater! Well, if it gives you pleasure, I will answer you. Man has both the spirit of good and the spirit of evil in him, that is to say, the possibility of doing the one or the other. If he succumbs to evil, he is damned. If he triumphs over it, he is rewarded. To be saved, he must earn salvation by struggling with all his powers."

"What powers?"

"Virtue and faith."

"And if he does not have enough virtue and faith, is that his fault?"

"Yes, because that comes from his having too much iniquity and blindness in his soul."

The man sat up again, seized by a new fit of anger which consumed him like a fever.

"Ah," he said, "original sin! There's nothing that can excuse the suffering of good people on earth. It is an abomination."

The priest looked at the rebellious man blankly.

"How else could souls be tried?" he said quite calmly.

"Nothing can excuse the suffering of the good."

"God's designs are inscrutable."

The dying man flung out his emaciated arms. His eyes became hollow.

"You are a liar!"

"Enough," said the priest. "I have listened patiently to your ramblings and feel sorry for you. But there's no good arguing. You must prepare to appear before God, from whom you seem to have lived apart. If you have suffered, you will be consoled in His bosom. Let that suffice for you."

The invalid fell back and lay still for a while. He remained motionless under the white spread, like a reclining sepulchral statue of marble with a face of bronze.

He regained his voice.

"God cannot console me."

"My son, my son, what are you saying?"

"God cannot console me, because He cannot give me what I want."

"Ah, my poor child, how far gone you are in your blindness! Why did you have me summoned?"

"I had hopes, I had hopes."

"Hopes? Hopes of what?"

"I do not know. The things we hope for are always the things we do not know."

His hands wavered in the air, then fell down again.

"Time is passing," said the priest and began all over again.

"Tell me the circumstances of your sin. Tell me. When you were alone with this person, when you two were close together, did you talk to each other, or did you keep quiet?"

"I do not believe in you," said the man.

The priest frowned.

"Repent, and tell me that you believe in the Catholic religion, which will save you."

But the other man shook his head in utter anguish and denied all his happiness.

"Religion—" he began.

The priest interrupted brutally.

"You are not going to start over again! Keep quiet. All your arguments are worthless. Begin by *believing* in religion and then you will see what it means. I have come to force you to believe."

It was a duel to the end. The two men at the edge of the grave glared at each other like enemies.

"You must believe."

"I do not believe."

"You must."

"You would make truth different from what it is by threats."

"Yes." He stressed the clear, elementary command. "Whether you are convinced or not, believe. Evidence does not count. The one important thing is faith. God does not deign to convince the incredulous. These are no longer the days of miracles. The only miracle is in our hearts, and it is faith. Believe!" He hurled the same word ceaselessly, like stones.

"My son," he continued, more solemnly, standing up, with his large fat hand uplifted, "I exact of you an act of faith."

"Get out!" said the man, with hatred.

But the priest did not stir. Goaded by the urgence of the case, impelled by the necessity of saving this soul in spite of itself, he became implacable.

"You are going to die," he said, "you are going to die. You have only a few more minutes to live. Submit."

"No," said the man.

The black-robed priest caught hold of both his hands.

"Submit. No discussion. You are losing precious time. All your reasoning is of no account. We are alone, you and I before God."

He shook his head with the low bulging forehead, the prominent fleshy nose, wide moist nostrils dark with snuff, thin yellow lips like twine tight across two projecting teeth that showed by themselves in the darkness. There were lines on his forehead and between his eyebrows and around his mouth. His cheeks and chin were covered with a grey layer.

"I represent God," he said. "You are in my presence as if you were in the presence of God. Simply say 'I believe,' and I will absolve you. 'I believe,' that is all. The rest makes no difference to me."

He bent lower and lower, almost gluing his face to that of the dying man, trying to plant his absolution like a blow.

"Simply say with me, 'Our Father, who art in heaven.' I do not ask you to do anything else."

The sick man's face contracted.

"No—no!"

Suddenly the priest rose with a triumphant air.

"At last! You have said it."

"No."

"Ah!" muttered the priest between his teeth.

He twisted the man's hands in his. You felt he would have put his arms around him to stifle him, assassinate him if his death rattle would have brought a confession—so possessed was he with the desire to persuade him, to snatch from him the words he had come to seek on his lips.

He let the withered hands go, paced the room like a wild beast, then came back and stationed himself in front of the bed again.

"Remember—you are going to die," he stammered to the miserable man. "You will soon be in the earth. Say, 'Our Father,' just these two words, nothing else."

He hung over him with his eyes on his mouth, his dark, crouching figure like a demon lying in wait for a soul, like the whole Church over dying humanity.

"Say it! Say it! Say it!"

The sick man tried to wrest himself free. There was a rattle of fury in his throat. With the remnant of his voice, in a low tone, he gasped:

"No!"

"Scoundrel!" cried the priest.

And he struck him in the face. After that neither man made a move for a while. Then the priest went at it again.

"At least you will die holding a crucifix," he snarled.

He drew a crucifix from his pocket, and put it down hard on his breast.

The other man shook himself in a dull horror, as if religion were contagious, and threw the crucifix on the floor.

The priest stooped, mumbling insults. "Carrion, you want to die like a dog, but I am here!" He picked up the crucifix, and with a gleam in his eyes, sure of crushing him, waited for his final chance.

The dying man panted, completely at the end of his strength. The priest, seeing him in his power, laid the crucifix on his breast again. This time the other man let it stay there, unable to do anything but look at it with eyes of hatred. But his eyes did not make it fall.

WHEN THE BLACK MAN HAD gone out into the night, and the patient little by little recovered from the struggle and felt free once more, it occurred to me that the priest in his violence and coarseness was horribly right. A bad priest? No, a good priest, who spoke strictly according to his conscience and belief, and tried to apply his religion simply, such as it was, without hypocritical concessions. Ignorant, clumsy, gross—yes, but honest and logical even in his fearful attempt. In the half-hour that I had listened to him, he had tried by all the means that religion uses and recommends to follow his calling of making converts and giving absolution. He had said everything that a priest cannot help saying. Every dogma had come out clearly and definitely from the mouth of this rough, common hewer of wood and drawer of water for his religion. If the sick man was right, so was the priest.

WHAT WAS THAT THING NEAR the bed, that thing which loomed so high and did not stir and had not been there a moment before? It stood between me and the leaping flame of the candle placed near the sick man.

I accidentally made a little noise in leaning against the wall, and very slowly the thing turned a face toward me with a frightened look on it that frightened me.

I knew that head. Was it not the landlord himself, a man with peculiar ways, whom we seldom saw?

He had been walking up and down the hall, waiting for the sick man to be left alone. And now he was standing beside him as he lay in bed either asleep or helpless from weakness.

He stretched his hand out toward a bag. In doing so, he kept his eyes on the dying man, so that his hand missed the bag twice.

There was a creaking on the floor above, and both the man and I trembled. A door slammed. He rose as if to keep back an exclamation.

He opened the bag slowly, and I, no longer myself, I was afraid that he would not have time.

He drew a package out of the bag. It made a slight sound. When he saw the roll of banknotes in his hand, I observed the extraordinary gleam on his face. All the sentiments of love were there, adoration, mysticism, and also brutal love, a sort of supernatural ecstasy and the gross satisfaction that was already tasting immediate joys. Yes, all the loves impressed themselves for a moment on the profound humanity of this thief's face.

Some one was waiting for him behind the half-open door. I saw an arm beckoning to him.

He went out on tiptoe, first slowly, then quickly.

I am an honest man, and yet I held my breath along with him. I *understood* him. There is no use finding excuses for myself. With a horror and a joy akin to his, I was an accomplice in his robbery.

All thefts are induced by passion, even that one, which was cowardly and vulgar. Oh, his look of inextinguishable love for the treasure suddenly snatched up. All offences, all crimes are outrages accomplished in the image of the immense desire for theft, which is the very essence and form of our naked soul.

Does that mean that we must absolve criminals, and that punishment is an injustice? No, we must protect ourselves. Since society rests upon honesty, we must punish criminals to reduce them to impotence, and above all to strike them with terror, and halt others on the threshold of evil deeds. But once the crime is established, we must not look for excuses for it. We run the danger then of always finding excuses. We must condemn it in advance, by virtue of a cold principle. Justice should be as cold as steel.

HENRI BARBUSSE

But justice is not a virtue, as its name seems to indicate. It is an organisation the virtue of which is to be feelingless. It does not aim at expiation. Its function is to establish warning examples, to make of the criminal a thing to frighten off others.

Nobody, nothing has the right to exact expiation. Besides, no one can exact it. Vengeance is too remote from the act and falls, so to speak, upon another person. Expiation, then, is a word that has no application in the world.

XIII

He was very, very weak and lay absolutely still and silent, chained fast by the baleful weight of his flesh. Death had already put an end to even his faintest quiverings.

His wonderful companion sat exactly where his fixed eyes fell on her, at the foot of the bed. She held her arms resting on the base board of the bed with her beautiful hands drooping. Her profile sloped downward slightly, that fine design, that delicate etching of eternal sweetness upon the gentle background of the evening. Under the dainty arch of her eyebrows her large eyes swam clear and pure, miniature skies. The exquisite skin of her cheeks and forehead gleamed faintly, and her luxuriant hair, which I had seen flowing, gracefully encircled her brow, where her thoughts dwelt invisible as God.

She was alone with the man who lay there as if already in his grave— she who had wished to cling to him by a thrill and to be his chaste widow when he died. He and I saw nothing on earth except her face. And in truth, there was nothing else to be seen in the deep shadows of the evening.

A voice came from the bed. I scarcely recognised it.

"I haven't said everything yet that I want to say," said the voice.

Anna bent over the bed as if it were the edge of a coffin to catch the words that were to issue for the last time, no doubt, from the motionless and almost formless body.

"Shall I have the time? Shall I?"

It was difficult to catch the whisper, which almost stuck in his throat. Then his voice accustomed itself to existence again and became distinct.

"I should like to make a confession to you, Anna. I do not want this thing to die with me. I am sorry to let this memory be snuffed out. I am sorry for it. I hope it will never die.

"I loved once before I loved you.

"Yes, I loved the girl. The image I have left of her is a sad, gentle one. I should like to snatch it from death. I am giving it to you because you happen to be here."

He gathered himself together to have a clear vision of the woman of whom he was speaking.

"She was fair-haired and fair-skinned," he said.

"You needn't be jealous, Anna. (People are jealous sometimes even when they are not in love.) It was a few years after you were born. You

HENRI BARBUSSE

were a little child then, and nobody turned to look at you on the streets except the mothers.

"We were engaged in the ancestral park of her parents. She had bright curls tied with ribbons. I pranced on horseback for her. She smiled for me.

"I was young and strong then, full of hope and full of the beginning of things. I thought I was going to conquer the world, and even had the choice of the means to conquer it. Alas, all I did was to cross hastily over its surface. She was younger than I, a bud so recently, blown, that one day, I remember, I saw her doll lying on the bench that we were sitting on. We used to say to each other, 'We shall come back to this park when we are old, shall we not?' We loved each other—you understand—I have no time to tell you, but you understand, Anna, that these few relics of memory that I give you at random are beautiful, incredibly beautiful.

"She died the very day in spring when the date of our wedding was set. We were both taken sick with a disease that was epidemic that year in our country, and she did not have the strength to escape the monster. That was twenty-five years ago. Twenty-five years, Anna, between her death and mine.

"And now here is the most precious secret, her name."

He whispered it. I did not catch it.

"Say it over again, Anna."

She repeated it, vague syllables which I caught without being able to unite them into a word.

"I confide the name to you because you are here. If you were not here, I should tell it to anyone, no matter whom, provided that would save it."

He added in an even, measured voice, to make it hold out until the end:

"I have something else to confess, a wrong and a misfortune."

"Didn't you confess it to the priest?" she asked in surprise.

"I hardly told him anything," was all he replied.

And he resumed, speaking calmly, with his full voice:

"I wrote poems during our engagement, poems about ourselves. The manuscript was named after her. We read the poems together, and we both liked and admired them. 'Beautiful, beautiful!' she would say, clapping her hands, whenever I showed her a new poem. And when we were together, the manuscript was always with us—the most beautiful book that had ever been written, we thought. She did not want the poems to be published and get away from us. One day in the garden she told me what she wanted. 'Never! Never!' she said over and over again, like an obstinate, rebellious child, tossing her dainty head with its dancing hair."

The man's voice became at once surer and more tremulous, as he filled in and enlivened certain details in the old story.

"Another time, in the conservatory, when it had been raining monotonously since morning, she asked, 'Philip'—she used to pronounce my name just the way you do."

He paused, himself surprised by the primitive simplicity of what he had just expressed.

"'Do you know,' she asked, 'the story of the English painter Rossetti?' and she told me the episode, which had so vividly impressed her, how Rossetti had promised the lady he loved to let her keep forever the manuscript of the book he had written for her, and if she died, to lay it beside her in her coffin. She died, and he actually carried out his promise and buried the manuscript with her. But later, bitten by the love of glory, he violated his promise and the tomb. 'You will let me have your book if I die before you, and will not take it back, will you, Philip?' And I promised laughingly, and she laughed too.

"I recovered from my illness slowly. When I was strong enough, they told me that she had died. When I was able to go out, they took me to the tomb, the vast family sepulchre which somewhere hid her new little coffin.

"There's no use my telling you how miserable I was and how I grieved for her. Everything reminded me of her. I was full of her, and yet she was no more! As I recovered from the illness, during which my memory had faded, each detail brought me a recollection. My grief was a fearful reawakening of my love. The sight of the manuscript brought my promise back to me. I put it in a box without reading it again, although I had forgotten it, things having been blotted out of my mind during my convalescence. I had the slab removed and the coffin opened, and a servant put the book in her hands.

"I lived. I worked. I tried to write a book. I wrote dramas and poems. But nothing satisfied me, and gradually I came to want our book back.

"I knew it was beautiful and sincere and vibrant with the two hearts that had given themselves to each other. Then, like a coward, three years afterward, I tried to re-write it—to show it to the world. Anna, you must have pity on us all! But I must say it was not only the desire for glory and praise, as in the case of the English artist, which impelled me to close my ears to the sweet, gentle voice out of the past, so strong in its powerlessness, 'You will not take it back from me, will you, Philip?' It was not only for the sake of showing off in a book of great beauty. It was also to refresh my memory, for all our love was in that book.

"I did not succeed in reconstructing the poems. The weakening of my faculties soon after they were written, the three years afterward during which I made a devout effort not to revive the poems even in thought, since they were not to keep on living—all this had actually wiped the book out of my mind. It was with difficulty that I recalled—and then only by chance—the mere titles of some of the poems, or a few of the verses. Of some parts, all I retained was just a confused echo. I needed the manuscript itself, which was in the tomb.

"One night, I felt myself going there.

"I felt myself going there after periods of hesitation and inward struggles which it is useless to tell you about because the struggles themselves were useless. I thought of the other man, of the Englishman, of my brother in misery and crime as I walked along the length of the cemetery wall while the wind froze my legs. I kept saying to myself it was not the same thing, and this insane assurance was enough to make me keep on.

"I asked myself if I should take a light. With a light it would be quick. I should see the box at once and should not have to touch anything else—but then I should see *everything!* I preferred to grope in the dark. I had rubbed a handkerchief sprinkled with perfume over my face, and I shall never forget the deception of this odour. For an instant, in the stupefaction of my terror, I did not recognise the first thing I touched—her necklace—I saw it again on her living body. The box! The corpse gave it to me with a squashing sound. Something grazed me faintly.

"I had meant to tell you only a few things, Anna. I thought I should not have time to tell you how everything happened. But it is better so, better for me that you should know all. Life, which has been so cruel to me, is kind at this moment when you are listening, you who will live. And my desire to express what I felt, to revive the past, which made of me a being accursed during the days I am telling you about, is a benefit this evening which passes from me to you, and from you to me."

The young woman was bending toward him attentively. She was motionless and silent. What could she have said, what could she have done, that would have been sweeter than her silent attention?

"The rest of the night I read the stolen manuscript. Was it not the only way to forget her death and think of her life?

"I soon saw that the poems were not what I had thought them to be.

"They game me a growing impression of being confused and much too lengthy. The book so long adored was no better than what I had done afterwards. I recalled, step by step, the background, the occasion, the vanished gesture that had inspired these verses, and in spite of their resurrection, I found them undeniably commonplace and extravagant.

"An icy despair gripped me, as I bent my head over these remains of song. Their sojourn in the tomb seemed to have deformed and crushed the life out of my verses. They were as miserable as the wasted hand from which I had taken them. They had been so sweet! 'Beautiful, beautiful!' the happy little voice had cried so many times while she clasped her hands in admiration.

"It was because her voice and the poems had been vibrating with life and because the ardour and delirium of our love had adorned my rhymes with all their charms, that they seemed so beautiful. But all that was past, and in reality our love was no more.

"It was oblivion that I read at the same time as I read my book. Yes, death had been contagious. My verses had remained there too long, sleeping down below there in awful peace—in the sepulchre into which I should never have dared to enter if love had still been alive. She was indeed dead.

"I thought of what a useless and sacrilegious thing I had done and how useless and sacrilegious everything is that we promise and swear to here below.

"She was indeed dead. How I cried that night. It was my true night of mourning. When you have just lost a beloved there is a wretched moment, after the brutal shock, when you begin to understand that all is over, and blank despair surrounds you and looms like a giant. That night was a moment of such despair when I was under the sway of my crime and the disenchantment of my poems, greater than the crime, greater than everything.

"I saw her again. How pretty she was, with her bright, lively ways, her animated charm, her rippling laugh, the endless number of questions she was always asking. I saw her again in the sunlight on the bright lawn. She was wearing a dress of old rose satin, and she bent over and smoothed the soft folds of her skirt and looked at her little feet. (Near us was the whiteness of a statue.) I remembered how once

I had for fun tried to find a single flaw in her complexion. Not a spot on forehead, cheek, chin—anywhere. Her skin was as smooth as if it had been polished. I felt as though that exquisite delicate face were something ever in flight that had paused for an instant for my sake, and I stammered, almost with tears in my voice, 'It is too much! It is too much!' Everybody looked on her as a princess. In the streets of the town the shopkeepers were glad to see her pass by. Did she not have a queenly air as she sat half-reclining on the great carved stone bench in the park, that great stone bench which was now a kind of empty tomb?

"For a moment in the midst of time I knew how much I had loved her, she who had been alive and who was dead, who had been the sun and who was now a kind of obscure spring under the earth.

"And I also mourned the human heart. That night I understood the extremes of what I had felt. Then the inevitable forgetfulness came, the time came when it did not sadden me to remember that I had mourned.

"THAT IS THE CONFESSION I wanted to make to you, Anna. I wanted this story of love, which is a quarter of a century old, never to end. It was so real and thrilling, it was such a big thing, that I told it to you in all simplicity, to you who will survive. After that I came to love you and I do love you. I offer to you as to a sovereign the image of the little creature who will always be seventeen."

He sighed. What he said proved to me once more the inadequacy of religion to comfort the human heart.

"Now I adore you and you alone—I who adored her, I whom she adored. How can there possibly be a paradise where one would find happiness again?"

His voice rose, his inert arms trembled. He came out of his profound immobility for a moment.

"Ah, *you* are the one, *you* are the one—*you* alone."

And a great cry of impotence broke from him.

"Anna, Anna, if you and I had been really married, if we had lived together as man and wife, if we had had children, if you had been beside me as you are this evening, but really beside me!"

He fell back. He had cried out so loud that even if there had been no breach in the wall, I should have heard him in my room. He voiced his whole dream, he threw it out passionately. This sincerity, which was indifferent to everything, had a definite significance which bruised my heart.

"Forgive me. Forgive me. It is almost blasphemy. I could not help it."

He stopped. You felt his will-power making his face calm, his soul compelling him to silence, but his eyes seemed to mourn.

He repeated in a lower voice, as if to himself, "You! You!"

He fell asleep with "You" on his lips.

He died that night. I saw him die. By a strange chance he was alone at the last moment.

There was no death rattle, no death agony, properly speaking. He did not claw the bedclothes with his fingers, nor speak, nor cry. No last sigh, no last flash.

He had asked Anna for a drink. As there was no more water in the room and the nurse happened to be away at that moment, she had gone out to get some quickly. She did not even shut the door.

The lamplight filled the room. I watched the man's face and felt, by some sign, that the great silence at that moment was drowning him.

Then instinctively I cried out to him. I could not help crying out so that he should not be alone.

"I see you!"

My strange voice, disused from speaking, penetrated into the room.

But he died at the very instant that I gave him my madman's alms. His head dropped back stiffly, his eyeballs rolled. Anna came in again. She must have caught the sound of my outcry vaguely, for she hesitated.

She saw him. A fearful cry burst from her with all the force of her healthy body, a true widow's cry. She dropped on her knees at the bedside.

The nurse came in right after her and raised her arms. Silence reigned, that flashing up of incredible misery into which you sink completely in the presence of the dead, no matter who you are or where you are. The woman on her knees and the woman standing up watched the man who was stretched there, inert as if he had never lived. They were both almost dead.

Then Anna wept like a child. She rose. The nurse went to tell the others. Instinctively, Anna, who was wearing a light waist, picked up a black shawl that the nurse had left on a chair and put it around her.

The room, so recently desolate, now filled with life.

They lit candles everywhere, and the stars, visible through the window, disappeared.

They knelt down, and cried and prayed to him. The dead man held command. "He" was always on their lips. Servants were there whom I had not yet seen but whom he knew well. These people around him all seemed to be lying, as though it was they who were suffering, they who were dying, and he were alive.

"He must have suffered a great deal when he died," said the doctor, in a low voice to the nurse, at a moment when he was quite near me.

"But he was so weak, the poor man!"

"Weakness does not prevent suffering except in the eyes of others," said the doctor.

THE NEXT MORNING THE DRAB light of the early day fell upon the faces and the melancholy funeral lights. The coming of the day, keen and cold, had a depressing effect upon the atmosphere of the room, making it heavier, thicker.

A voice in a low apologetic tone for a moment interrupted the silence that had lasted for hours.

"You mustn't open the window. It isn't good for the dead body."

"It is cold," some one muttered.

Two hands went up and drew a fur piece close. Some one rose, and then sat down again. Some one else turned his head. There was a sigh.

It was as if they had taken advantage of these few words to come out of the calm in which they had been concealed. Then they glanced once more at the man on the bier—motionless, inexorably motionless.

I must have fallen asleep when all at once I heard the church bells ringing in the grey sky.

After that harassing night there was a relaxation from rigid attention to the stillness of death, and an inexplicable sweetness in the ringing of the bells carried me back forcibly to my childhood. I thought of the countryside where I used to hear the bells ringing, of my native land, where everything was peaceful and good, and the snow meant Christmas, and the sun was a cool disk that one could and should look at.

The tolling of the bells was over. The echo quietly died away, and then the echo of the echo. Another bell struck, sounding the hour. Eight o'clock, eight sonorous detached strokes, beating with terrible regularity, with invincible calm, simple, simple. I counted them, and when they had ceased to pulsate in the air, I could not help counting them over again. It was time that was passing—formless time, and the human effort that defined it and regularized it and made of it a work as of destiny.

XIV

I was alone. It was late at night, and I was sitting at my table. My lamp was buzzing like summer in the fields. I lifted my eyes. The stars studded the heavens above. The city was plunged at my feet. The horizon escaped from nearby into eternity. The lights and shadows formed an infinite sphere around me.

I was not at ease that night. I was a prey to an immense distress. I sat as if I had fallen into my chair. As on the first day I looked at my reflection in the glass, and all I could do was just what I had done then, simply cry, "I!"

I wanted to know the secret of life. I had seen men, groups, deeds, faces. In the twilight I had seen the tremulous eyes of beings as deep as wells. I had seen the mouth that said in a burst of glory, "I am more sensitive than others." I had seen the struggle to love and make one's self understood, the refusal of two persons in conversation to give themselves to each other, the coming together of two lovers, the lovers with an infectious smile, who are lovers in name only, who bury themselves in kisses, who press wound to wound to cure themselves, between whom there is really no attachment, and who, in spite of their ecstasy deriving light from shadow, are strangers as much as the sun and the moon are strangers. I had heard those who could find no crumb of peace except in the confession of their shameful misery, and I had seen faces pale and red-eyed from crying. I wanted to grasp it all at the same time. All the truths taken together make only one truth. I had had to wait until that day to learn this simple thing. It was this truth of truths which I needed.

Not because of my love of mankind. It is not true that we love mankind. No one ever has loved, does love, or will love mankind. It was for myself, solely for myself, that I sought to attain the full truth, which is above emotion, above peace, even above life, like a sort of death. I wanted to derive guidance from it, a faith. I wanted to use it for my own good.

I went over the things I had seen since living in the boarding-house. They were so numerous that I had become a stranger to myself. I scarcely had a name any more. I fairly listened to the memory of them, and in supreme concentration I tried to see and understand what I was. It would be so beautiful to know who I was.

I thought of all those wise men, poets, artists before me who had suffered, wept, and smiled on the road to truth. I thought of the Latin poet who wished to reassure and console men by showing them truth as unveiled as a statue. A fragment of his prelude came to my mind, learned long ago, then dismissed and lost like almost everything that I had taken the pains to learn up till then. He said he kept watch in the serene nights to find the words, the poem in which to convey to men the ideas that would deliver them. For two thousand years men have always had to be reassured and consoled. For two thousand years I have had to be delivered. Nothing has changed the surface of things. The teachings of Christ have not changed the surface of things, and would not even if men had not ruined His teachings so that they can no longer follow them honestly. Will the great poet come who shall settle the boundaries of belief and render it eternal, the poet who will be, not a fool, not an ignorant orator, but a wise man, the great inexorable poet? I do not know, although the lofty words of the man who died in the boarding-house have given me a vague hope of his coming and the right to adore him already.

But what about me—me, who am only a glance from the eye of destiny? I am like a poet on the threshold of a work, an accursed, sterile poet who will leave no glory behind, to whom chance *lent* the truth that genius would have *given* him, a frail work which will pass away with me, mortal and sealed to others like myself, but a sublime work nevertheless, which will show the essential outlines of life and relate the drama of dramas.

WHAT AM I? I AM the desire not to die. I have always been impelled—not that evening alone—by the need to construct the solid, powerful dream that I shall never leave again. We are all, always, the desire not to die. This desire is as immeasurable and varied as life's complexity, but at bottom this is what it is: To continue to *be*, to *be* more and more, to develop and to endure. All the force we have, all our energy and clearness of mind serve to intensify themselves in one way or another. We intensify ourselves with new impressions, new sensations, new ideas. We endeavour to take what we do not have and to add it to ourselves. Humanity is the desire for novelty founded upon the fear of death. That is what it is. I have seen it myself. Instinctive movements, untrammelled utterances always tend the same way, and the most dissimilar utterances are all alike.

HENRI BARBUSSE

But afterwards! Where are the words that will light the way? What is humanity in the world, and what is the world?

Everything is within me, and there are no judges, and there are no boundaries and no limits to me. The *de profundis*, the effort not to die, the fall of desire with its soaring cry, all this has not stopped. It is part of the immense liberty which the incessant mechanism of the human heart exercises (always something different, always!). And its expansion is so great that death itself is effaced by it. For how could I imagine my death, except by going outside of myself, and looking at myself as if I were not I but somebody else?

We do not die. Each human being is alone in the world. It seems absurd, contradictory to say this, and yet it is so. But there are many human beings like me. No, we cannot say that. In saying that, we set ourselves outside the truth in a kind of abstraction. All we can say is: I am alone.

And that is why we do not die.

Once, bowed in the evening light, the dead man had said, "After my death, life will continue. Every detail in the world will continue to occupy the same place quietly. All the traces of my passing will die little by little, and the void I leave behind will be filled once more."

He was mistaken in saying so. He carried all the truth with him. Yet we, *we* saw him die. He was dead for us, but not for himself. I feel there is a fearfully difficult truth here which we must get, a formidable contradiction. But I hold on to the two ends of it, groping to find out what formless language will translate it. Something like this: "Every human being is the whole truth." I return to what I heard. We do not die since we are alone. It is the others who die. And this sentence, which comes to my lips tremulously, at once baleful and beaming with light, announces that death is a false god.

But what of the others? Granted that I have the great wisdom to rid myself of the haunting dread of my own death, there remains the death of others and the death of so many feelings and so much sweetness. It is not the conception of truth that will change sorrow. Sorrow, like joy, is absolute.

And yet! The infinite grandeur of our misery becomes confused with glory and almost with happiness, with cold haughty happiness. Was it out of pride or joy that I began to smile when the first white streaks of dawn turned my lamp pale and I saw I was alone in the universe?

XV

It was the first time I had seen her in mourning, and that evening her youth shone more resplendent than ever.

Her departure was close at hand. She looked about to see if she had left anything behind in the room, which had been made ready for other people, the room which was already formless, already abandoned.

The door opened. The young woman turned her head. A man appeared in the sunny doorway.

"Michel, Michel, Michel!" she cried.

She stretched out her arms, hesitated, and for a few seconds remained motionless as light, with her full gaze upon him.

Then, in spite of where she was and the purity of her heart and the chastity of her whole life, her legs shook and she was on the verge of falling over.

He threw his hat on the bed with a sweeping romantic gesture. He filled the room with his presence, with his weight. His footsteps made the floor creak. He kept her from falling. Tall as she was, he was a whole head taller. His marked features were hard and remarkably fine. His face under a heavy head of black hair was bright and clean, as though new. He had a drooping moustache and full red lips.

He put his hands on the young woman's shoulders, and looked at her, in readiness for his eager embrace.

They held each other close, staggering. They said the same word at the same time, "At last!" That was all they said, but they said it over and over again in a low voice, chanting it together. Their eyes uttered the same sweet cry. Their breasts communicated it to each other. It seemed to be tying them together and making them merge into one. At last! Their long separation was over. Their love was victor. At last they were together. And I saw her quiver from head to foot. I saw her whole body welcome him while her eyes opened and then closed on him again. They made a great effort to speak to each other. The few shreds of conversation held them back a moment.

"How I waited for you! How I longed for you!" he stammered. "I thought of you all the time. I saw you all the time. Your smile was everywhere." He lowered his voice and added, "Sometimes when people were talking commonplaces and your name happened to be mentioned, it would go through my heart like an electric current."

He panted. His deep voice burst into sonorous tones. He seemed unable to speak low.

"Often I used to sit on the brick balustrade at the top of the terrace of our house overlooking the Channel, with my face in my hands, wondering where you were. But it did not matter how far away you were, I could not help seeing you all the same."

"And often I," said Anna, bending her head, "would sit at the open window warm evenings, thinking of you. Sometimes the air was of a suffocating sweetness, as it was two months ago at the Villa of the Roses. Tears would come to my eyes."

"You used to cry?"

"Yes," she said in a low voice, "for joy."

Their mouths joined, their two small purple mouths of exactly the same colour. They were almost indistinguishable from each other, tense in the creative silence of the kiss, a single dark stream of flesh.

Then he drew away a little to get a better look at her, and the next moment caught her in his arms and held her close.

His words fell on her like hammer blows.

"Down there the scent of the sap and the flowers from the many gardens near the coast used to intoxicate me, and I wanted to burrow my fingers in the dark burning earth. I would roam about and try to remember your face, and draw in the perfume of your body. I would stretch my arms out in the air to touch as much as possible of your sunlight."

"I knew you were waiting for me and that you loved me," she said, in a voice gentler but just as deep with emotion. "I saw you in your absence. And often, when the light of dawn entered my room and touched me, I thought of how completely consecrated I was to your love. Thinking of you sometimes in my room in the evening, I would admire myself."

A thrill went through him, and he smiled.

He kept saying the same things in scarcely different words, as if he knew nothing else. He had a childish soul and a limited mind behind the perfect sculpture of his forehead and his great black eyes, in which I saw distinctly the white face of the woman floating like a swan.

She listened to him devoutly, her mouth half open, her head thrown back lightly. Had he not held her, she would have slipped to her knees before this god who was as beautiful as she.

"The memory of you saddened my joys, but consoled my sorrows."

I did not know which of the two said this. They embraced vehemently. They reeled. They were like two tall flames. His face burned hers, and he cried:

"I love you, I love you! All through my sleepless nights of longing for you—oh, what a crucifixion my solitude was!

"Be mine, Anna!"

She radiated consent, but her eyes faltered, and she glanced round the room.

"Let us respect this room," she breathed. Then she was ashamed at having refused, and immediately stammered, "Excuse me."

The man also looked around the room. His forehead darkened with a savage frown of suspicion, and the superstition of his race shone in his eyes.

"It was here—that he died?"

"No," she said.

AFTERWARDS THEY DID AS THE others had done, as human beings always do, as they themselves would do many times again in the strange future—they sat with their eyes half-closed and the same uneasy look of shame and terror in them as Amy and her lover.

But these two required no artificial stimulus for their love. They had no need of the night. And they felt no culpability. They were two grand young creatures, driven together naturally by the very force of their love, and their ardour cleansed everything, like fire. They were innocent. They had no regrets and felt no remorse. They thought they were united.

He took her soft hand in his dark hand, and said: "Now you are mine for always. You have made me know divine ecstasy. You have my heart and I have yours. You are my wife forever."

"You are everything to me," she answered.

They went forth into life like a couple in legend, inspired and rosy with anticipation—he, the knight with no shadows falling on him except the dark of his hair, helmeted or plumed, and she, the priestess of the pagan gods, the spirit of nature.

They would shine in the sunlight. They would see nothing around them, blinded by the daylight. They would undergo no struggles except the strife of the sexes and the spying of jealousy; for lovers are enemies rather than friends.

I followed them with my eyes going through life, which would be nothing to them but fields, mountains, or forests. I saw them veiled in a

HENRI BARBUSSE

kind of light, sheltered from darkness, protected for a time against the fearful spell of memory and thought.

I sat down and leaned on my elbows. I thought of myself. Where was I now after all this? What was I going to do in life? I did not know. I would look about and would surely find something.

So, sitting there, I quietly indulged in hopes. I must have no more sadness, no more anguish and fever. If the rest of my life was to pass in calm, in peace, I must go far, far away from all those awful serious things, the sight of which was terrible to bear.

Somewhere I would lead a wise, busy life—and earn my living regularly.

And you, you will be beside me, my sister, my child, my wife.

You will be poor so as to be more like all other women. In order for us to be able to live together I shall work all day and so be your servant. You will work affectionately for us both in this room, and in my absence there will be nothing beside you but the pure, simple presence of your sewing machine. You will keep the sort of order by which nothing is forgotten, you will practice patience which is as long as life, and maternity which is as heavy as the world.

I shall come in, I shall open the door in the dark, I shall hear you come from the next room, bringing the lamp. A dawn will announce you. You will tell me the quiet story of your day's work, without any object except to give me your thoughts and your life. You will speak of your childhood memories. I shall not understand them very well because you will be able to give me, perforce, only insufficient details, but I shall love your sweet strange language.

We shall speak of the child we shall have, and you will bend your head and your neck, white as milk, and in our minds we shall hear the rocking of the cradle like a rustling of wings. And when we are tired out, and even after we have grown old, we shall dream afresh along with our child.

After this revery our thoughts will not stray, but linger tenderly. In the evening we shall think of the night. You will be full of a happy thought. Your inner life will be gay and shining, not because of what you see, but because of your heart. You will beam as blind people beam.

We shall sit up facing each other. But little by little, as it gets late, our words will become fewer and less intelligible. Sleep will lay bare your soul. You will fall asleep over the table, you will feel me watching over you more and more.

Tenderness is greater than love. I do not admire carnal love when it is by itself and bare. I do not admire its disorderly selfish paroxysms, so grossly short-lived. And yet without love the attachment of two human beings is always weak. Love must be added to affection. The things it contributes to a union are absolutely needed—exclusiveness, intimacy, and simplicity.

XVI

I went out on the street like an exile, I who am an everyday man, who resemble everybody else so much, too much. I went through the streets and crossed the squares with my eyes fixed upon things without seeing them. I was walking, but I seemed to be falling from dream to dream, from desire to desire. A door ajar, an open window gave me a pang. A woman passing by grazed against me, a woman who told me nothing of what she might have told me. I dreamed of her tragedy and of mine. She entered a house, she disappeared, she was dead.

I stood still, a prey to a thousand thoughts, stifled in the robe of the evening. From a closed window on the ground floor floated a strain of music. I caught the beauty of a sonata as I would catch distinct human words, and for a moment I listened to what the piano was confiding to the people inside.

Then I sat down on a bench. On the opposite side of the avenue lit by the setting sun two men also seated themselves on a bench. I saw them clearly. They seemed overwhelmed by the same destiny, and a mutual sympathy seemed to unite them. You could tell they liked each other. One was speaking, the other was listening.

I read a secret tragedy. As boys they had been immensely fond of each other. They had always been of the same mind and shared their ideas. One of them got married, and it was the married one who was now speaking. He seemed to be feeding their common sorrow.

The bachelor had been in the habit of visiting his home, always keeping his proper distance, though perhaps vaguely loving the young wife. However, he respected her peace and her happiness. The married man was telling him that his wife had ceased to love him, while he still adored her with his whole being. She had lost interest in him, and turned away from him. She did not laugh and did not smile except when there were other people present. He spoke of this grief, this wound to his love, to his right. His right! He had unconsciously believed that he had a right over her, and he lived in this belief. Then he found out that he had no right.

Here the friend thought of certain things she had said to him, of a smile she had given him. Although he was good and modest and still perfectly pure, a warm, irresistible hope insinuated itself into his heart. Listening to the story of despair that his friend confided to him, he raised his face bit by bit and gave the woman a smile. And nothing could keep that evening, now falling grey upon those two men, from being at once an end and a beginning.

A couple, a man and a woman—poor human beings almost always go in pairs—approached, and passed. I saw the empty space between them. In life's tragedy, separation is the only thing one sees. They had been happy, and they were no longer happy. They were almost old already. He did not care for her, although they were growing old together. What were they saying? In a moment of open-heartedness, trusting to the peacefulness reigning between them at that time, he owned up to an old transgression, to a betrayal scrupulously and religiously hidden until then. Alas, his words brought back an irreparable agony. The past, which had gently lain dead, rose to life again for suffering. Their former happiness was destroyed. The days gone by, which they had believed happy, were made sad; and that is the woe in everything.

This couple was effaced by another, a young one, whose conversation I also imagined. They were beginning, they were going to love. Their hearts were so shy in finding each other. "Do you want me to go on that trip?" "Shall I do this and that?" She answered, "No." An intense feeling of modesty gave this first avowal of love so humbly solicited the form of a disavowal. But yet they were already thinking of the full flower of their love.

Other couples passed by, and still others. This one now—he talking, she saying nothing. It was difficult for him to master himself. He begged her to tell him what she was thinking of. She answered. He listened. Then, as if she had said nothing, he begged her again, still harder, to tell him. There he was, uncertain, oscillating between night and day. All he needed was for her to say one word, if he only believed it. You saw him, in the immense city, clinging to that one being. The next instant I was separated from these two lovers who watched and persecuted each other.

Turn where you will, everywhere, the man and the woman ever confronting each other, the man who loves a hundred times, the woman who has the power to love so much and to forget so much. I went on my way again. I came and went in the midst of the naked truth. I am not a man of peculiar and exceptional traits. I recognise myself in everybody. I have the same desires, the same longings as the ordinary human being. Like everybody else I am a copy of the truth spelled out in the Room, which is, "I am alone and I want what I have not and what I shall never have." It is by this need that people live, and by this need that people die.

But now I was tired of having desired too much. I suddenly felt old. I should never recover from the wound in my breast. The dream of peace that I had had a moment before attracted and tempted me only because it was far away. Had I realised it, I should simply have dreamed another dream.

Now I looked for a word. The people who live my truth, what do they say when they speak of themselves? Does the echo of what I am thinking issue from their mouths, or error, or falsehood?

Night fell. I looked for a word like mine, a word to lean upon, a word to sustain me. And it seemed to me that I was going along groping my way as if expecting some one to come from round the corner and tell me everything.

I did not return to my room. I did not want to leave the crowds that evening. I looked for a place that was alive.

I went into a large restaurant so as to hear voices around me. There were only a few vacant places, and I found a seat in a corner near a table at which three people were dining. I gave my order, and while my eyes mechanically followed the white-gloved hand pouring soup into my plate from a silver cup, I listened to the general hubbub.

All I could catch was what my three neighbours were saying. They were talking of people in the place whom they knew, then of various friends. Their persiflage and the consistent irony of their remarks surprised me.

Nothing they said was worth the while, and the evening promised to be useless like the rest.

A few minutes later, the head waiter, while serving me with filets of sole, nodded his head and winked his eye in the direction of one of the guests.

"M. Villiers, the famous writer," he whispered proudly.

I recognised M. Villiers. He resembled his portraits and bore his young glory gracefully. I envied that man his ability to write and say what he thought. I studied his profile and admired its worldly distinction. It was a fine modern profile, the straightness of it broken by the silken point of his well-kept moustache, by the perfect curve of his shoulder, and by the butterfly's wing of his white necktie.

I lifted my glass to my lips when suddenly I stopped and felt all my blood rush to my heart.

This is what I heard:

"What's the theme of the novel you're working on?"

"Truth," replied Pierre Villiers.

"What?" exclaimed his friend.

"A succession of human beings caught just as they are."

"What subject?" somebody asked.

People turned and listened to him. Two young diners not far away stopped talking and put on an idling air, evidently with their ears pricked. In a sumptuous purple alcove, a man in evening clothes, with sunken eyes and drawn features, was smoking a fat cigar, his whole life concentrated in the fragrant glow of his tobacco. His companion, her bare elbow on the table, enveloped in perfume and sparkling with jewels, and overloaded with the heavy artificiality of luxury, turned her simple moon-like face toward the speaker.

"This is the subject," said Pierre Villiers. "It gives me scope to amuse and tell the truth at the same time. A man pierces a hole in the wall of a boarding-house room, and watches what is going on in the next room."

I MUST HAVE LOOKED AT the speakers just then with a rather sorry expression of bewilderment. Then I quickly lowered my head like a child afraid to be seen.

They had spoken for *me,* and I sensed a strange secret service intrigue around me. Then, in an instant this impression, which had got the better of my common sense, gave way. Evidently a pure coincidence. Still I was left with the vague apprehension that they were going to notice that I *knew,* and were going to recognise me.

One of the novelist's friends begged him to tell more of his story. He consented.

He was going to tell it in my presence!

WITH ADMIRABLE ART IN THE use of words, gestures, and mimicry, and with a lively elegance and a contagious laugh, he described a series of brilliant, surprising scenes. Under cover of his scheme, which brought all the scenes out into peculiar relief and gave them a special intensity, he retailed a lot of amusing oddities, described comical persons and things, heaped up picturesque and piquant details, coined typical and witty proper names, and invented complicated and ingenious situations. He succeeded in producing irresistible effects, and the whole was in the latest style.

They said, "Ah!" and "Oh!" and opened their eyes wide.

"Bravo! A sure success! A corking funny idea!"

"All the characters who pass before the eyes of the man spying upon them are amusing, even the man who kills himself. Nothing forgotten. The whole of humanity is there."

But I had not recognized a single thing in the entire show.

A stupor and a sort of shame overwhelmed me as I heard that man trying to extract the utmost entertainment possible from the dark happenings that had been torturing me for a month.

I thought of that great voice, now silenced, which had said so clearly and forcefully that the writers of today imitate the caricaturists. I, who had penetrated into the heart of humanity and returned again, found nothing human in this jiggling caricature! It was so superficial that it was a lie.

He said in front of me—of me the awful witness:

"It is man stripped of all outward appearances that I want people to see. Others are fiction, I am the truth."

"It has a philosophical bearing, too."

"Perhaps. But that wasn't my object. Thank God, I am a writer, and not a thinker."

And he continued to travesty the truth, and I was impotent—the truth, that profound thing whose voice was in my ears, whose shadow was in my eyes, and whose taste was in my mouth.

Was I so utterly forsaken? Would no one speak the word I was in search of?

THE ROOM WAS FLOODED WITH moonlight. In that magnificent setting there was an obscure white couple, two silent human beings with marble faces.

The fire was out. The clock had finished its work and had stopped, and was listening with its heart.

The man's face dominated. The woman was at his feet. They did nothing. An air of tenderness hovered over them. They looked like monuments gazing at the moon.

He spoke. I recognised his voice. It lit up his face for me, which had been shrouded from my sight before. It was *he*, the nameless lover and poet whom I had seen twice before.

He was telling Amy that on his way that evening he had met a poor woman, with her baby in her arms.

She walked, jostled and borne along by the crowd returning home from work, and finally was tossed aside up against a post under a porch, and stopped as though nailed there.

"I went up to her," he said, "and saw she was smiling."

"WHAT WAS SHE SMILING AT? At life, on account of her child. Under the refuge where she was cowering, facing the setting sun, she was thinking of the growth of her child in the days to come. However terrible they might be, they would be around him, for him, in him. They would be the same thing as her breath, her walk, her look.

"So profound was the smile of this creator who bore her burden and who raised her head and gazed into the sun, without even looking down at the child or listening to its babbling.

"I worked this woman and child up into a poem."

He remained motionless for a moment, then said gently without pausing, in that voice from the Beyond which we assume when we recite, obeying what we say and no longer mastering it:

"The woman from the depths of her rags, a waif, a martyr—smiled. She must have a divine heart to be so tired and yet smile. She loved the sky, the light, which the unformed little being would love some day. She loved the chilly dawn, the sultry noontime, the dreamy evening. The child would grow up, a saviour, to give life to everything again. Starting at the dark bottom he would ascend the ladder and begin life over again, life, the only paradise there is, the bouquet of nature. He would make beauty beautiful. He would make eternity over again with his voice and his song. And clasping the new-born infant close, she looked at all the sunlight she had given the world. Her arms quivered like wings. She dreamed in words of fondling. She fascinated all the passersby that looked at her. And the setting sun bathed her neck and head in a rosy reflection. She was like a great rose that opens its heart to the whole world."

The poet seemed to be searching for something, to be seeing things, and believing infinitely. He was in another world where everything we see is true and everything we say is unforgettable.

Amy was still on her knees with eyes upraised to his. She was all attention, filled with it like a precious vase.

"But her smile," he went on, "was not only in wonder about the future. There was also something tragic in it, which pierced my heart. I understood it perfectly. She adored life, but she detested men and was afraid of them, always on account of the child. She already disputed over him with the living, although he himself was as yet scarcely among the living. She defied them with her smile. She seemed to say to them, 'He will live in spite of you, he will use you, he will subdue you either to dominate you or to be loved by you. He is already braving you with his tiny breath, this little one that I am holding in my maternal grasp.' She was terrible. At first, I had seen her as an angel of goodness. Now, although she had not changed, she was like an angel of mercilessness and vengeance. I saw a sort of hatred for those who would trouble him distort her face, resplendent with superhuman maternity. Her cruel heart was full of one heart only. It foresaw sin and shame. It hated men and settled accounts with them like a destroying angel. She was the mother with fearful nails, standing erect, and laughing with a torn mouth."

Amy gazed at her lover in the moonlight. It seemed to me that her looks and his words mingled.

"I come back as I always do to the greatness of mankind's curse, and I repeat it with the monotony of those who are always right—oh, without God, without a harbour, without enough rags to cover us, all we have, standing erect on the land of the dead, is the rebellion of our smile, the rebellion of being gay when darkness envelops us. We are divinely alone, the heavens have fallen on our heads."

The heavens have fallen on our heads! What a tremendous idea! It is the loftiest cry that life hurls. That was the cry of deliverance for which I had been groping until then. I had had a foreboding it would come, because a thing of glory like a poet's song always gives something to us poor living shadows, and human thought always reveals the world. But I needed to have it said explicitly so as to bring human misery and human grandeur together. I needed it as a key to the vault of the heavens.

These heavens, that is to say, the azure that our eyes enshrine, purity, plenitude—and the infinite number of suppliants, the sky of truth and religion. All this is within us, and has fallen upon our heads. And God Himself, who is all these kinds of heavens in one, has fallen on our heads like thunder, and His infinity is ours.

We have the divinity of our great misery. And our solitude, with its toilsome ideas, tears and laughter, is fatally divine. However wrong we may go in the dark, whatever our efforts in the dark and the useless work of our hearts working incessantly, and whatever our ignorance left to itself, and whatever the wounds that other human beings are, we ought to study ourselves with a sort of devotion. It is this sentiment that lights our foreheads, uplifts our souls, adorns our pride, and, in spite of everything, will console us when we shall become accustomed to holding, each at his own poor task, the whole place that God used to occupy. The truth itself gives an effective, practical, and, so to speak, religious caress to the suppliant in whom the heavens spread.

"I HAVE SUCH RESPECT FOR the actual truth that there are moments when I do not dare to call things by their name," the poet ended.

"Yes," said Amy, very softly, and nothing else. She had been listening intently. Everything seemed to be carried away in a sort of gentle whirlwind.

"Amy," he whispered.

She did not stir. She had fallen asleep with her head on her lover's knees. He looked at her and smiled. An expression of pity and benevolence flitted across his face. His hands stretched out part way toward the sleeping woman with the gentleness of strength. I saw the glorious pride of condescension and charity in this man whom a woman prostrate before him deified.

XVII

I have given notice. I am going away tomorrow evening, I with my tremendous memory. Whatever may happen, whatever tragedies may be reserved for me in the future, my thought will not be graver or more important when I shall have lived my life with all its weight.

But my whole body is one pain. I cannot stand on my legs any more. I stagger. I fall back on my bed. My eyes close and fill with smarting tears. I want to be crucified on the wall, but I cannot. My body becomes heavier and heavier and filled with sharper pain. My flesh is enraged against me.

I hear voices through the wall. The next room vibrates with a distant sound, a mist of sound which scarcely comes through the wall.

I shall not be able to listen any more, or look into the room, or hear anything distinctly. And I, who have not cried since my childhood, I cry now like a child because of all that I shall never have. I cry over lost beauty and grandeur. I love everything that I should have embraced.

Here they will pass again, day after day, year after year, all the prisoners of rooms will pass with their kind of eternity. In the twilight when everything fades, they will sit down near the light, in the room full of haloes. They will drag themselves to the window's void. Their mouths will join and they will grow tender. They will exchange a first or a last useless glance. They will open their arms, they will caress each other. They will love life and be afraid to disappear. Here below they will seek a perfect union of hearts. Up above they will seek everlastingness among the shades and a God in the clouds.

The monotonous murmur of voices comes through the wall steadily, but I do not catch what is being said. I am like anybody else in a room.

I am lost, just as I was the evening I came here when I took possession of this room used by people who had disappeared and died—before this great change of light took place in my destiny.

Perhaps because of my fever, perhaps because of my lofty pain, I imagine that some one there is declaiming a great poem, that some one is speaking of Prometheus. He has stolen light from the gods. In his entrails he feels the pain, always beginning again, always fresh, gathering from evening to evening, when the vulture steals to him as it would steal to its nest. And you feel that we are all like Prometheus because of desire, but there is neither vulture nor gods.

There is no paradise except that which we create in the great tomb of the churches. There is no hell, no inferno except the frenzy of living.

There is no mysterious fire. I have stolen the truth. I have stolen the whole truth. I have seen sacred things, tragic things, pure things, and I was right. I have seen shameful things, and I was right. And so I have entered the kingdom of truth, if, while preserving respect to truth and without soiling it, we can use the expression that deceit and religious blasphemy employ.

WHO SHALL COMPOSE THE BIBLE of human desire, the terrible and simple Bible of that which drives us from life to life, the Bible of our doings, our goings, our original fall? Who will dare to tell everything, who will have the genius to see everything?

I believe in a lofty form of poetry, in the work in which beauty will be mingled with beliefs. The more incapable of it I feel myself, the more I believe it to be possible. The sad splendour with which certain memories of mine overwhelm me, shows me that it is possible. Sometimes I myself have been sublime, I myself have been a masterpiece. Sometimes my visions have been mingled with a thrill of evidence so strong and so creative that the whole room has quivered with it like a forest, and there have been moments, in truth, when the silence cried out.

But I have stolen all this, and I have profited by it, thanks to the shamelessness of the truth revealed. At the point in space in which, by accident, I found myself, I had only to open my eyes and to stretch out my mendicant hands to accomplish more than a dream, to accomplish almost a work.

What I have seen is going to disappear, since I shall do nothing with it. I am like a mother the fruit of whose womb will perish after it has been born.

What matter? I have heard the annunciation of whatever finer things are to come. Through me has passed, without staying me in my course, the Word which does not lie, and which, said over again, will satisfy.

BUT I HAVE FINISHED. I am lying stretched out, and now that I have ceased to see, my poor eyes close like a healing wound and a scar forms over them.

And I seek assuagement for myself. I! The last cry, as it was the first.

HENRI BARBUSSE

As for me, I have only one recourse, to remember and to believe. To hold on with all my strength to the memory of the tragedy of the Room.

I believe that the only thing which confronts the heart and the reason is the shadow of that which the heart and the reason cry for. I believe that around us there is only one word, the immense word which takes us out of our solitude, NOTHING. I believe that this does not signify our nothingness or our misfortune, but, on the contrary, our realisation and our deification, since everything is within us.

THE END

A NOTE ABOUT THE AUTHOR

Henri Barbusse (1873–1935) was a novelist and member of the French Communist Party. Born in Asnières-sur-Seine, he moved to Paris at 16. There, he published his first book of poems, *Pleureuses* (1895) and embarked on a career as a novelist and biographer. In 1914, at the age of 41, Barbusse enlisted in the French Army to serve in the First World War, for which he would earn the Croix de guerre. His novel *Under Fire* (1916) was inspired by his experiences in the war, which scarred him and influenced his decision to become a pacifist. In 1918, he moved to Moscow, where he joined the Bolshevik Party and married a Russian woman. Barbusse briefly returned to France, joining the French Communist Party in 1923, before moving back to Russia to work as a writer whose purpose was to support Bolshevism, illuminate the dangers of capitalism, and inspire revolutionary movements worldwide. In addition to his writing, Barbusse took part in the World Committee Against War and Fascism and the International Youth Congress, as well as worked as an editor for *Monde, Progrès Civique,* and *L'Humanité.* His final work was a biography of Joseph Stalin, which appeared in 1936 after his death from pneumonia in Moscow. Buried in Paris, his funeral was attended by a half million mourners. Among his many friends and colleagues were Egon Kisch, Albert Einstein, and Romain Rolland.

A NOTE FROM THE PUBLISHER

Spanning many genres, from non-fiction essays to literature classics to children's books and lyric poetry, Mint Edition books showcase the master works of our time in a modern new package. The text is freshly typeset, is clean and easy to read, and features a new note about the author in each volume. Many books also include exclusive new introductory material. Every book boasts a striking new cover, which makes it as appropriate for collecting as it is for gift giving. Mint Edition books are only printed when a reader orders them, so natural resources are not wasted. We're proud that our books are never manufactured in excess and exist only in the exact quantity they need to be read and enjoyed.

Discover more of your favorite classics with Bookfinity™.

- Track your reading with custom book lists.
- Get great book recommendations for your personalized Reader Type.
- Add reviews for your favorite books.
- AND MUCH MORE!

Visit **bookfinity.com** and take the fun Reader Type quiz to get started.

Enjoy our classic and modern companion pairings!